WINE COUNTRY COURIER

Community Buzz

The Ashton saga comes to a close!

Mystery finally solved. At long last, the murderer of Spencer Ashton has been named and arrested. Who would have imagined it was his own daughter, Grace Ashton? Thankfully she and her no-good husband are behind bars and the Ashton family can finally breathe a sigh of relief.

Yet the battle for the Ashton fortune rages on. Half brothers Eli and Trace are still going head to head to determine who are the rightful heirs. Will this billion-dollar dynasty ever be sorted out? Trace is as hard-hearted as his father, but he might be lightening up if the rumors are true that Becca Marshall has returned to Napa Valley. Wasn't the Ashton golden boy once engaged to this girl from the wrong side of the tracks? And wasn't there a rumor floating about that Spencer Ashton had bought off his son's unsuitable bride-to-be? With Spencer long buried, will Trace and Becca also be able to lay the past to rest?

I can't wait to find out how it all ends!

Dear Reader,

Celebrate the conclusion of 2005 with the six fabulous novels available this month from Silhouette Desire. You won't be able to put down the scintillating finale to DYNASTIES: THE ASHTONS once you start reading Barbara McCauley's *Name Your Price.* He believes she was bought off by his father...she can't fathom his lack of trust. Neither can deny the passion still pulsing between them.

We are so excited to have Caroline Cross back writing for Desire...and with a brand-new miniseries, MEN OF STEELE. In *Trust Me,* reunited lovers have more to deal with than just relationship troubles—they are running for their lives. Kristi Gold kicks one out of the corral as she wraps up TEXAS CATTLEMAN'S CLUB: THE SECRET DIARY with her story of secrets and scandals, *A Most Shocking Revelation.*

Enjoy the holiday cheer found in Joan Elliott Pickart's *A Bride by Christmas,* the story of a wedding planner who believes she's jinxed never to be a bride herself. Anna DePalo is back with another millionaire playboy who finally meets his match, in *Tycoon Takes Revenge.* And finally, welcome brand-new author Jan Colley to the Desire lineup with *Trophy Wives,* a story of lies and seduction not to be missed.

Be sure to come back next month when we launch a new and fantastic twelve-book family dynasty, THE ELLIOTTS.

Melissa Jeglinski

Melissa Jeglinski
Senior Editor
Silhouette Books

BARBARA McCAULEY

Name Your Price

Published by Silhouette Books
America's Publisher of Contemporary Romance

Special thanks and acknowledgment are given to Barbara McCauley for her contribution to the DYNASTIES: THE ASHTONS series.

To Terry and Marla Sutherland who made this book a joy to write! You guys are the best!

SILHOUETTE BOOKS

ISBN 0-373-76693-9

NAME YOUR PRICE

This edition published by arrangement with Harlequin Books S.A.

Visit Silhouette Books at www.eHarlequin.com

Printed in U.S.A.

Books by Barbara McCauley

Silhouette Desire

Woman Tamer #621
Man from Cougar Pass #698
Her Kind of Man #771
Whitehorn's Woman #803
A Man like Cade #832
Nightfire #875
**Texas Heat* #917
**Texas Temptation* #948
**Texas Pride* #971
Midnight Bride #1028
The Nanny and the Reluctant Rancher #1066
Courtship in Granite Ridge #1128
Seduction of the Reluctant Bride #1144
†*Blackhawk's Sweet Revenge* #1230
†*Secret Baby Santos* #1236
†*Killian's Passion* #1242
†*Callan's Proposition* #1290
†*Reese's Wild Wager* #1360
Fortune's Secret Daughter #1390
†*Sinclair's Surprise Baby* #1402
†*Taming Blackhawk* #1437
†*In Blackhawk's Bed* #1447
Royally Pregnant #1480
†*That Blackhawk Bride* #1491
Where There's Smoke... #1507
The Cinderella Scandal #1555
†*Miss Pruitt's Private Life* #1593
Name Your Price #1693

Silhouette Intimate Moments

†*Gabriel's Honor* #1024

Silhouette Books

Summer Gold
Wolf River Summer

Summer in Savannah
"Under Cover of the Night"

†*Blackhawk Legacy*

*Hearts of Stone
†Secrets!

BARBARA McCAULEY,

who has written more than thirty novels for Silhouette Books, lives in Southern California with her own handsome hero husband, Frank, who makes it easy to believe in and write about the magic of romance. Barbara's stories have won and been nominated for numerous awards, including the prestigious RITA® Award from the Romance Writers of America, Best Desire of the Year from *Romantic Times BOOKclub* and Best Short Contemporary from the National Reader's Choice Awards.

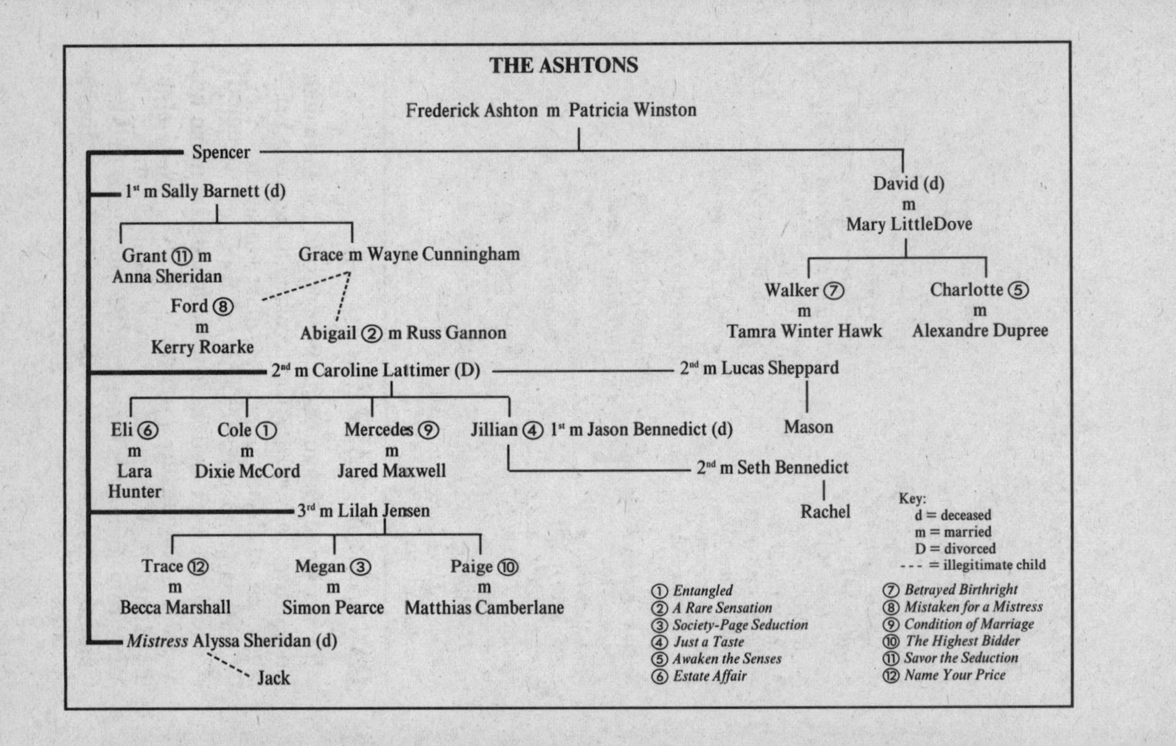
THE ASHTONS
Frederick Ashton m Patricia Winston
Spencer
David (d)
m
Mary LittleDove
1st m Sally Barnett (d)
Grant ⑪ m
Anna Sheridan
Grace m Wayne Cunningham
Ford ⑧
m
Kerry Roarke
Abigail ② m Russ Gannon
Walker ⑦
m
Tamra Winter Hawk
Charlotte ⑤
m
Alexandre Dupree
2nd m Caroline Lattimer (D)
2nd m Lucas Sheppard
Eli ⑥
m
Lara
Hunter
Cole ①
m
Dixie McCord
Mercedes ⑨
m
Jared Maxwell
Jillian ④ 1st m Jason Bennedict (d)
Mason
2nd m Seth Bennedict
Rachel
3rd m Lilah Jensen
Trace ⑫
m
Becca Marshall
Megan ③
m
Simon Pearce
Paige ⑩
m
Matthias Camberlane
Mistress Alyssa Sheridan (d)
Jack
Key:
d = deceased
m = married
D = divorced
- - - = illegitimate child
① Entangled
② A Rare Sensation
③ Society-Page Seduction
④ Just a Taste
⑤ Awaken the Senses
⑥ Estate Affair
⑦ Betrayed Birthright
⑧ Mistaken for a Mistress
⑨ Condition of Marriage
⑩ The Highest Bidder
⑪ Savor the Seduction
⑫ Name Your Price

Prologue

Spencer Ashton knew he was going to die.

Before this moment, he had never considered his own death. Arrogance and pride had refused to allow him the possibility of his own demise. After all, at sixty-two years young, he was a man still in his prime. A virile, handsome man, wealthy beyond his wildest dreams. He had everything he'd ever wanted and more. Fast cars, elegant homes, any woman he desired. The son of a lowly farmer and mousy wife from Podunk, Nebraska, he had done damn well for himself. If he'd happened to step on a few insignificant people along the way, what did that matter to him?

It hadn't, until he felt the bullet explode through his chest.

Astonished, Spencer looked up at the lowlife, greasy-haired slime who'd pulled the trigger, Wayne Cunningham, then he turned his gaze to the woman beside him.

His own flesh and blood.

Her eyes glinted green ice as she stared back.

Spencer glanced down at the hand he'd clutched to his heart and saw the blood seeping through his fingers. Warm, deep red, it trickled down his three-hundred-dollar silk Armani tie.

He tried to speak, but the only thing he managed was a strangled whisper.

"What's that you say, Daddy, dear?" Hatred dripped like acid from every word. She moved closer to the leather desk chair where Spencer sat dying, a sneer on her bright red lips as she leaned in close. "Cat got your tongue?"

"Grace—" He managed the single word, then started to choke on the blood filling his lungs.

"All I ever wanted was a fair share of what was mine. I had a right," she snarled, hitting her chest with her fist before she whirled away. "I *earned* the right, dammit! Grant and me were barely out of the womb when you left us. We had nothing, *nothing*."

She dragged her hands through the sides of her brown hair and continued to rant. "Our mother died of a broken heart because of you, and not once did you ever think of her, or the babies you abandoned. While we lived off church charity and wore second-hand rags, you were living in a mansion, eating gourmet meals in expensive restaurants with your fancy new wife and the four brats she gave you."

Spencer stared at his daughter through the haze of pain clouding his eyes. He'd paid the stupid bitch and her husband off for years so they'd keep quiet about his first marriage to her mother in Nebraska. But now that everyone knew he'd been married to Sally and never divorced her, Spencer had seen no reason to pay one more penny of blackmail money. For all it mattered now, Grace and her lame excuse for a husband could hire a band and parade it through town with a banner that said Spencer Ashton was a bigamist.

When Wayne had pulled out the gun, Spencer had never dreamed the sniveling idiot would actually have the guts to use it.

It was an error in calculation he would pay for with his life.

Wayne shifted nervously. "Gracie, baby, we should go before someone comes."

"The office has been closed for an hour and everyone's gone home." A smile lifted one corner of her mouth as she swiveled a look back at Spencer. "No one's coming."

"Baby, I know, but still—"

"We'll go when I'm through, dammit, and not before," Grace snapped, her smile gone. She leaned across her father's desk and stared into his eyes. Eyes the same color as her own. "And all that wasn't even enough for you, you greedy, coldhearted bastard. You had to have it all, so you stole everything from her, too, then tossed them all out like yesterday's garbage and married yet again."

Lilah. His third wife, probably the only woman who had truly understood him, Spencer thought. The only woman who had been as ambitious as he. She'd been a decent wife, a handsome woman in her younger years. She'd given him a son and two daughters, had even tolerated his affairs—until the last one, which had resulted in a child.

Little Jack. A son that Spencer knew he'd never see grow up.

"Now you'll pay, you son of a bitch," Spencer

heard Grace say, though her voice seemed to come from somewhere far away.

Cold slithered through his veins. Time seemed to slow as the darkness crept along the edges of his vision. And with that darkness came an awareness, an understanding that Grace was right, and he must now make restitution for the things he'd done in his life. All at once, every sin he'd committed flashed through his mind, a fast-forward motion picture of faces and images…

So many…he thought.

And with his last breath, as the icy darkness closed over him, Spencer Ashton knew he would rot in hell forever.

One

He should have seen it coming.

Trace had known, of course, that she was in town. He'd heard her name whispered behind his back on more than one occasion in the past few days, had heard the murmurs and seen the fleeting glances flashed in his direction. Becca Marshall returning to Napa Valley was like rich compost to the gossip-mongers, and the grapevine was sending out runners and suckers as if it were April instead of December.

Trace pursed his lips, knew that the fruit of that vine would most certainly be sour.

He still wasn't sure what had snagged his attention to the linen-draped table inside the little main street café. Maybe the tumble of thick, coffee-dark hair against the white turtleneck she wore, or maybe the familiar slash of high cheekbones and straight nose. Maybe even the graceful gesture of her long fingers as she spoke to another person who was just out of his line of sight.

No, it was none of those things, he thought as he stared at Becca. Because before he'd stopped on the sidewalk, before he'd glanced across the street, before he'd spotted her through the restaurant window, he'd simply known she was there. As surely as the scent of cinnamon and spices drifting from Katie's Country Bakery, as surely as the persistent ring of the handheld bell from the Santa Claus around the corner, as surely as the promise of rain on the cool evening air, he'd felt her presence.

The realization brought with it a flash of dark anger, but he quickly tamped down the emotion. It didn't matter one damn bit if she'd come back. The past was the past. Ancient history. Hell, they'd both been kids back then. He'd just turned twenty-one, she'd been twenty. He'd teased her she couldn't even legally drink. She'd teased him that he was an old man.

With all that had happened in the past few months,

his father's murder, his half-sister's arrest and confession, the family altercations and feuds—God knew on more than one occasion he'd certainly felt like an old man.

And now Becca.

He stepped under the black-cloth awning of a closed antique store and stared through the café window, noted that the five years that had passed since he'd last seen Becca had been good to her. The soft shine of colored Christmas lights decorating the restaurant window gave her skin an ethereal glow and lit her wide, thickly lashed eyes. Eyes the color of rich, golden-brown velvet, he remembered. Just one of the many memories associated with Becca. The throaty sound of her laugh, the heat of her long, smooth body sliding over his, the honey taste of her lips.

A taste now bitter with betrayal.

An icy breeze slid under the leather jacket he wore, but it did nothing to cool the heat simmering in his gut. He'd come to town to have dinner with his sister, for God's sake, not take a trip down memory lane.

He watched Becca's lips curve into a smile, saw the flash of dimple in her cheek. Grinding his teeth, he stepped back onto the sidewalk and crossed the street.

* * *

The sound of sleigh bells and the clomp of hooves on asphalt greeted Becca when she walked out of the restaurant into the cool night air. She watched a horse-drawn carriage pass by on the street, smiled at the driver when he lifted his top hat to her. Bundled in coats and hats, the man and woman in the rear seat waved and shouted a holiday greeting.

Christmas in Napa Valley had always been a magical time of year. Twinkling lights on every storefront, the animated reindeer and Santa on the roof of McIntye Hardware, the giant decorated tree in the center of Old Town. She breathed in the scent of pine and woodsmoke and crisp night air.

It felt good to be home.

Slipping her hands into her coat pockets, she walked down the sidewalk and took it all in. A few of the businesses had changed since she'd left five years ago. Emily's Bed and Linen was now The Blushing Bride bridal salon, Old Town Vintage Gifts was now Très Chic Fashion and Britwell's Tea Shop had expanded into a restaurant.

Change was inevitable, of course. You could fight it, you could deny it, you could even walk away from it. But no matter how hard you tried, you couldn't stop it.

Change was simply life.

The sound of music and a bell ringing drew Becca to a storefront of a small gift shop, and she paused to watch a two-foot-tall dancing snowman in the window. He wore a burgundy and deep green jeweled jester hat and vest and shook a tiny bell to the tune of "Jingle Bell Rock." A little redheaded girl standing inside the store laughed and pointed excitedly at the animated snowman.

Thank goodness there were at least a few things that didn't change, she thought, watching the excitement in the child's eyes. She'd felt that rush of excitement once, had felt that same joy.

Turning, she bumped into a man, felt his hands reach out and steady her.

"I'm so—"

She froze.

Oh dear God.

Even in the dim light, she knew the man's eyes were bottle-green, knew his hair was sandy-brown. Knew that he had a one-inch scar over his left eyebrow, the repercussion of a tree-climbing incident when he was eleven years old. Brow furrowed, his mouth pressed into a thin, hard line, he stared down at her with narrowed eyes.

"Hello, Becca."

Trace.

She'd known there was a strong possibility she might run into him while she was in Napa, though she'd certainly never imagined she would *literally* run into him. She'd spent weeks preparing herself for this moment, visualized herself remaining calm, composed. In control. She'd scripted exactly what she would say, exactly how she would smile. She'd even practiced the tone of her voice.

A tone that sounded nothing like the faint gasp she'd just uttered.

"Trace." She finally managed to whisper his name.

His hands still held her arms and she fought back the bubble of panic rising in her throat. Even through her coat, she felt the heat radiate from his body and seep into her skin. Her heart jackhammered against her ribs, reverberated in her head. How ridiculous she'd been to think she could have ever prepared herself to face him again.

How stupid.

When he finally dropped his hands away and stepped back, she managed to drag much needed air into her lungs. "I—I'm sorry," she said breathlessly. "I didn't see you."

"I heard you were back."

Afraid he might see how badly her hands were shaking, she thrust them deep into her pockets. "I'm here on a shoot for Ivy Glen Cellars."

"I heard that, too."

"Oh." She really wasn't surprised. The wine business in Napa was a close-knit community. She couldn't help but wonder what else he'd heard. And how much of it was true.

"How—how are you?" How trite and ridiculous the question sounded, Becca thought, but it seemed to be the best she could do at the moment.

"Fine. And you?"

"I'm good."

"It's been a long time, Becca."

Five years, she nearly said, but simply nodded instead. She noticed the fine lines around the corners of his eyes, the strong, square cut of his jaw, the hard set of his mouth, and was surprised at how the years had matured his handsome features. He'd once dazzled her with his boyish charm and crooked smile, but there was nothing welcoming in this man's expression.

A shiver coursed through her as she held his gaze. One thing hadn't changed, she thought with despair. He still made her knees weak. Still made her pulse flutter. Still made her yearn.

She was aware of the cars driving past, heard the bell still ringing from the gift store window, but her surroundings had a fuzzy, distant quality to them. Only Trace felt in focus, and her senses were sharply aware of every familiar detail. The broad stretch of shoulders, the dark slash of his brow, the slight crook in his nose.

Five years ago she would have jumped into his arms, laughing, then kissed him soundly. Five years ago he would have smiled and kissed her back, whispered something lustful in her ear that would have thrilled her—and made her blush.

The sound of the gift shop door opening shook Becca out of the trance she'd slipped into. A woman loaded down with brightly wrapped packages stepped onto the sidewalk, studying her watch as she hurried past. Becca glanced down, then took in a slow breath and looked back up at Trace.

"I'm sorry about your father," she said. Seven months ago, every newspaper and TV station in Los Angeles had carried the story of Spencer Ashton's murder. "I wanted to call you when I heard, but…"

Becca turned at the sound of the sleigh bells again. The carriage was on the other side of the street now, unloading its passengers.

Trace didn't even seem to notice. "But what?"

I was a coward. "I didn't want to intrude."

"I see."

The sarcasm in his voice cut her to the core. She wanted to reach out to him, tell him that he didn't see at all, but instead she simply hugged her coat closer. She couldn't bear to have him pull away from her.

"I really didn't think my condolences would be appreciated," she said quietly. "Especially considering what happened between us."

His mouth pressed into a hard line. "It wasn't *us*, Becca. You were the one who left."

He was right, of course. But standing on the sidewalk, with people and cars passing by in plain sight, it hardly seemed like the place to have this conversation. But then, she realized there wouldn't be *any* place she'd want to have this conversation. "Trace, please."

He stared at her for a long moment. Five years ago she could have read his eyes, known what he was thinking, what he was feeling. Not anymore. The years had changed him, she realized. He was a different man, one she barely recognized. And she was a different woman.

"I heard your mother bought the pub," Trace said unexpectedly.

"She'd been running the place for the past fifteen

years anyway." Grateful for the change in subject, Becca managed a smile. "It only made sense that Joseph would sell to her when he retired. She's having a grand opening next week."

She knew she was babbling now. Trace and his family owned one of the largest and most successful wineries in Napa Valley. Why would he even be remotely interested in a grand opening for Elaine Marshall's beer pub?

"You staying with her?"

"Just for two or three weeks, while I'm working on this project."

"Ivy Glen's a first-rate winery," he stated. "You must have impressed them."

They both knew how incredibly difficult it was to break into product photography work in Napa Valley, especially for a design company that hadn't already established a track record. "I'm happy they're giving me a chance."

When he said nothing, just continued to stare at her with those piercing green eyes of his, she shifted awkwardly. She didn't think her nerves could take any more of this superficial, polite conversation. "I should be going."

Nodding, he stepped aside. "Take care, Becca."

"You, too, Trace."

Somehow, on legs that felt like rubber, she managed to hold herself upright and walk, not run, away.

Fists in his pockets, Trace stood outside The Cask and Cleaver and waited for the knot in stomach to unwind.

Idiot.

What the hell had he been thinking? That somehow, magically, if he walked right up to her, if he looked her in the eyes and had a civil conversation with her, that all the anger he'd carried since she'd left would suddenly disappear?

It hadn't. If anything, he'd only made it worse. Made that knuckled fist in his gut colder, tighter.

Would it have mattered to him if she'd have made an attempt to apologize? he wondered. He considered it, then shook his head. No. It wouldn't have mattered. It might have even made him more angry.

You were the one who left, he'd reminded her, and for a moment, before she'd looked away, he'd almost thought he'd seen regret in her eyes. Guilt, he supposed. Five years ago she'd left him with a note and the engagement ring he'd placed on her finger only a month earlier. He'd stood there in disbelief, staring at her letter in disbelief until the words became lasered into his brain. *I'm sorry, Trace, but I have an opportunity to study photography in Milan, and I must follow my dream. I hope that someday you will find it in your heart to forgive me. I wish you all the best, always.*

What a fool he'd been to think that her dream had been to be his wife and the mother of his children.

Even now, after all this time, even after what she'd done, she still got to him. When she'd bumped into him and he'd held her arms, it had taken every ounce of strength not to pull her against him.

I should have, he thought, clenching his jaw. *I should have dragged her into my arms and kissed her senseless, then walked away.*

"Hey, mister, you got the time?"

Two teenage girls in knitted hats and scarfs passing by on the sidewalk jarred Trace out of his thoughts. He glanced at his watch. *Damn.* "Seven-twenty."

"Thanks. Merry Christmas," the girls said in unison, then hurried off, giggling and looking back at him over their shoulders.

Good grief, it was bad enough he was standing around thinking about Becca, now he had high school girls flirting with him. He scrubbed a hand over his face, knew he had to pull it together or Paige would know something was off.

"Good evening, Mr. Ashton." The hostess smiled a greeting when Trace stepped into the dimly lit restaurant. "Your sister is waiting for you."

"Thanks, Cindy."

Shrugging out of his overcoat, Trace followed the pretty blonde to a corner booth where Paige was busy studying a menu. The scent of butter-grilled steaks filled the oak-paneled room and the light of flickering votives cast shadows on thick oak tables. An instrumental version of "White Christmas" drifted from unseen speakers.

"Jim Beam, straight up, please," Trace told the hostess, then gave his sister a peck on the cheek and slid into the booth across from her. "Sorry I'm late."

"No need to be." Paige picked up the glass of red wine on the table. "I just got here myself. It's not easy shopping for the man who has everything."

A woman in love, Trace thought, glancing at his sister. Paige, with her soft brown hair and sparkling hazel-green eyes, had a pretty glow about her he'd never seen before. "I'm not that hard to buy for, am I?"

"You know perfectly well I'm talking about Matt," she said, lifting one brow. "I have no idea what he wants."

"Save your time and money." Trace glanced at the

glittering engagement diamond on Paige's left hand. "He's already got what he wants."

Smiling, Paige stared at the ring. "We both do. I love him so much, Trace."

"You set the date yet?"

"June, I think, but that doesn't give me much time to plan."

"Six months isn't enough time?" Trace shook his head. "I've never understood how it could take so long to prepare for a ten minute ceremony and a four hour party."

"That's because you're a man," she said, smiling while she sipped her wine. "Wait until you get married, then you'll understand."

"Not gonna happen, sis." He made an X with his index fingers and, eager to change the subject, asked, "Now you want to tell me why you suddenly had to see me tonight?"

"I saw Jack today."

Jack was their two-year-old half-brother, the last of the ten children that Spencer Ashton had fathered. Little Jack's mother had been Spencer's mistress, but the woman had died and the boy's aunt Anna had come to Napa with her nephew. "Paige—"

"Just hear me out." Paige reached across the table and took her brother's hand. "He's so adorable. He's got a smile that could melt an iceberg. He's exactly what we all need, Trace, the one thing that could pull this entire family together."

Sweet Paige, Trace thought with a sigh. Always the peacemaker. "We have seven half-brothers and -sisters, Paige, six of them abandoned by our father before he married our mother and raised us. You honestly think that one child could possibly bring us all together?"

"Come with me to visit him, Trace." Paige squeezed his hand. "Get to know him."

"You seem to forget I already tried that," Trace said sourly. "If I step foot on The Vines estate again, Eli will probably sick the dogs on me."

"*You* seem to forget the last time Eli came to the winery," Paige reminded him. "You greeted the man with a fist to his jaw."

"So maybe I overreacted a little," Trace admitted reluctantly. Eli had given back as good as he'd taken, and they'd both come away bruised and a little bloody that day.

The hostess returned with Trace's drink and Paige waited until the woman had left, then leaned forward and arched a brow. "You overreacted a *little?*"

"Okay, fine." Frowning, Trace tossed back a swallow of the whiskey, felt it burn all the way to his stomach. "So I overreacted a lot. Satisfied?"

"I'll be satisfied when you put a stop to this feud."

It surprised Trace how different his youngest sister had become since she'd met her fiancé. More confident, more determined. Both qualities he admired, but not when they were being used against him, he decided.

"Does our mother know you're making alliances with the enemy?" he asked.

"They're not the enemy, Trace," Paige said softly. "They're family. And like it or not, we share blood. If you'd at least give them a chance, you might actually like them. And as far as our mother goes, you know perfectly well she'd throw a tantrum if she found out I was visiting Jack or any of those 'people' as she so delicately calls them."

A tantrum would be putting it mildly, Trace thought. Lilah Ashton had made it abundantly clear to all three of her children that they were to have nothing to do with their half-sisters and -brothers or with Louret Vineyards, the winery that Spencer's second wife, Caroline, had started after their divorce. Trace knew—hell, *everyone* knew—that his mother was afraid she might have to share her late husband's fortune with the children of his first two marriages.

"Please, Trace," Paige pleaded. "Just tell me you'll think about it."

"Fine." He sighed and took another swallow of whiskey. "I'll think about it."

"Thank you." Paige clinked her glass against Trace's, then leaned back, sipping her wine while she studied him. "So now are you going to tell me?"

"Tell you what?"

"About Becca."

His hand tightened around the glass in his hand, then he casually set the drink back down. "What about Becca?"

"I saw you talking to her." Paige kept her hazel-green gaze on him.

Dammit, anyway. Wouldn't it figure that Paige had seen him? "We crossed paths. No big deal."

"You just saw the woman you were going to marry for the first time in five years." Paige lightly swirled the wine in her glass. "You don't think that's a big deal?"

He resisted the urge to down the rest of his whiskey. "No, I don't."

"I heard she's in town for a few weeks."

"Did you?" Trace did his best to look bored.

"Do you plan on seeing her while she's here?"

"No, I do not."

"You should, you know."

"Is that so?" *Where the hell was their waitress?*

he wondered, and glanced around the restaurant. "Why is that?"

"Lots of reasons," Paige said. "One, to give her a chance to explain why she left like she did."

"You know exactly why she left," Trace said through gritted teeth.

Paige stared at her wine thoughtfully. "You should at least hear it from her."

Bad idea. "You have another reason?"

"Closure," she said with a shrug. "Or a new beginning."

Just what he needed from his little sister. Advice on his personal life. "For God's sake, Paige. It's been five years. We've both moved on. End of story. Period."

Blissfully, the waitress showed up at that moment and, Paige, smart woman that she was, let the subject drop.

He didn't need closure, and he sure as hell didn't need a new beginning, Trace thought, only half listening to the menu specials for the evening.

When it came to Becca, he didn't need a damn thing.

Two

Still wearing her robe, Becca stood at the kitchen window and watched a soft rain dampen the juniper bushes and sidewalk lining her mother's front lawn. A steady *drip, drip, drip* of water from the eaves broke the early morning stillness, but it was a good sound, she thought. A calming sound.

Lord knew she needed a little calm.

Turning from the window, she dragged both hands through her tangled hair, scooped grounds into the coffeemaker, added water and flipped it on. After a night of restless sleep and disturbing dreams, she also needed a little caffeine.

While the coffeepot hissed and sputtered, Becca moved to the small round kitchen table in the corner of the room and slid her fingertips over the curved top of an oak chair. How many times had she sat here in this very chair with Trace and talked until the early hours of the morning? How many cups of coffee had they shared, how many dreams?

How many kisses?

She closed her eyes on a sigh, then dropped her hand away. Too many to count, she thought.

Just thinking about Trace's kiss sent a ripple of heat up her spine. He was the only man who'd ever made her feel that way. The only man who'd made her heart race and her knees weak. She supposed every woman looked back on her first love with those same feelings, but he hadn't simply been her first love. He'd been her only love.

"You're up early."

Startled, Becca turned at the sound of her mother's voice. She stood in the doorway, her reading glasses tucked neatly into the thick mass of brown hair she'd clipped on top of her head and a stack of file folders in her arms. Even at forty-two, Elaine Marshall hadn't a speck of gray, though the corners of her soft hazel eyes had tiny lines. She was an attractive woman, compact—five feet tall if she stretched her neck—and with a coat on, almost a hundred pounds. Dynamo was the word most people used to describe her. She had endless energy and Becca, in her entire life, couldn't remember a night her mother had slept more than six hours.

Apparently last night was no exception, Becca thought, noticing that her mother was dressed in the same white, long-sleeved blouse and black slacks she'd worn to work the day before. "And you're up late."

Becca had grown up with her mother working nights, but still, five-thirty in the morning was unusually late to be coming home.

"Inventory." With a tired smile, Elaine moved into the kitchen, dropped her files on the counter, then opened a cupboard and pulled out two mugs. "If I never hear *ninety-nine bottles of beer on the wall* again, it will be too soon."

Chuckling, Becca took the mugs from her mother. "I'll get you a cup."

"You don't need to—"

"I know I don't need to." Becca set the cups down and nudged her mother toward the kitchen table. "I want to."

"But—"

"Sit," Becca said more firmly.

Elaine started for the table, then turned and moved toward the pantry. "I've got some cinnamon rolls I can put in—"

"Mother, *sit.*"

Elaine raised an eyebrow. "Well, you certainly have gotten bossy."

"I learned it from you." Becca pulled out a chair. "Now put your butt down and let someone else wait on you for a change."

Sulking, Elaine sat. "You're not too old to paddle, you know."

Becca set a sugar bowl and spoon on the table, filled two mugs with coffee and set one in front of her mother. "You never paddled me once in my entire life."

"Obviously that's where I went wrong." Mouth set in a pout, Elaine poured two generous spoonfuls of sugar into her mug and stirred. She'd given up smoking ten years ago and replaced nicotine with sweets. It more than annoyed most people that she never gained an ounce. "Maybe you wouldn't have such a smart mouth on you if I had."

"I learned that from you, too." With her own cup in her hand, sans the sugar, Becca sat across from her mother. "Didn't I tell you I wanted to help you with inventory?"

"You've already got a job. And I seem to recall you had a dinner meeting last night, too."

"My meeting was over by eight." Becca looked at her mother and sighed. "Mom, I hardly see you anymore. I just want to help."

"I know, sweetie." Elaine patted her daughter's hand. "But really, I don't need any help. I've got everything under control."

Becca noticed the smudge of dark circles under her mother's eyes and the slight droop of her shoulders. Some people might consider Elaine Marshall a martyr. She'd worked 24/7 her entire adult life, too proud to ever ask anyone for help, including her own daughter. Becca knew her mother's fierce need for control wasn't born from a desire to be a saint, but from the seventeen-year-old girl who'd been pregnant and abandoned twenty-five years ago, a young woman fiercely determined to make it on her own and protect her child from the outside world.

Becca also knew there was no point in arguing it. Stubborn was her mother's middle name.

"Tell me about your meeting last night with Whitestone Winery," Elaine said, effectively changing the subject. "Was it successful?"

"I don't know yet. They're going to call me today." Since she'd seen Trace, Becca hadn't even thought about the account she'd hoped to get with the winery. "They're considering me to shoot an ad for a Chardonnay they're introducing next summer."

"They'll hire you. You're brilliant."

"You have to say that." Becca shook her head, but still, the words made her smile. "You're my mom."

"I say it because it's true." Elaine gave an all-knowing shrug. "You were ten years old when you took your first picture and even then you had a gift. And that you did *not* learn from me. To this day I don't know which end of a camera is up."

Her mother had always been her biggest champion, had always told her that if she believed, she could do anything or be anyone she wanted.

And Becca *had* believed, until she'd lost the one thing she'd wanted more than anything else.

She stared at her coffee, watched the steam slowly rise and the overhead light ripple on the dark liquid surface.

"You want to tell me?"

Becca glanced up. "Tell you what?"

Like only a mother could, Elaine tilted her head and raised a brow, but said nothing.

On a sigh, Becca looked away, let a few moments of silence pass until she finally said, "I saw Trace last night."

Now it was Elaine's turn to let the silence hover. She held her coffee mug with both hands and took a long sip, then carefully set the mug back on the table. "And?"

For the past five years, and even after Spencer's murder, Becca's mother had blatantly avoided any discussion regarding Trace. It was almost as if she avoided saying his name, she thought she could erase the past and her daughter's hurt.

"And nothing." Becca shrugged a shoulder. "I ran into him when I came out of the restaurant. He said hello, I said hello. He mentioned he'd heard you'd bought the pub, I told him I was sorry about his father. That was it."

"Are you going to see him again?"

It was a simple question, but the unspoken concern, the objection, weighed heavy in Elaine's voice. Irritation flashed through Becca. "If you mean *see*, as in get together, no. Look, Mom, if you're worried about me and Trace—"

"Did I say I was worried?"

Becca could have argued, could have told her mother that she didn't have to say a word, that she'd never had to say a word. Becca had always known her mother hadn't approved of her engagement to Trace any more than Trace's mother and father had approved.

It had been a fantasy to ever think that she and Trace could have been happy when the odds had been so completely stacked against them.

Becca pushed away from the table and stood. "I've got to get ready for work."

Elaine reached for her daughter's arm. "Becca, I'm sorry—"

"It's all right. I shouldn't have brought it up now." Becca sighed, then smiled and kissed her mother's forehead. "Go get some sleep, Mom. You look tired."

White lights sparkled in the great hall at Ivy Glen Cellars. On the twelve-foot Christmas tree, on the garland-draped windows, across the wide doorways. Poinsettias, a mix of deep red and creamy white, filled the corners and brightened the food tables. Over the animated buzz of conversation and the clink of wineglasses, a quartet played Tchaikovsky's "Dance of the Sugar Plum Fairies."

A glass of Cabernet in his hand, Trace stood on the sidelines and looked out over the sea of people. He knew quite a few of the faces, a mix of local vintners, restaurant owners and distributors. The holiday luncheon was to showcase Ivy Glen's latest harvest, and though it was a party, to Trace it was also work.

"Trace." Reed Vale, Ivy Glen's general manager,

stepped out of the crowd and held out a hand. In the Valley, Reed was known as much for his business acumen as he was for his golden-boy looks. "Glad you could make it."

Trace smiled and shook Reed's hand. He was one of the few men that Trace thought of as a friend. "Gotta keep an eye on the competition."

"Which is exactly why I'll be at your barrel sampling next week." Reed nodded at the glass of wine in Trace's hand. "So what do you think?"

It was good, actually. Very good. The color, aroma and finish were excellent. But because Trace had known Reed since they were kids, he couldn't pass up an opportunity to annoy him. "Not bad."

"Coming from you, I'll take that as a compliment," Reed said with a cocky grin, snagging a toothpick-speared bite of cheese from a pretty redhead passing a tray. "By the way, in case you hadn't already heard, we hired Becca Marshall to shoot a layout for our spring catalog."

Trace kept his face impassive and glanced around the busy room, nodded at a restaurant manager from Sonoma who kept a healthy stock of Ashton Estate labels. "I heard."

"She's good, Trace." Reed washed his cheese down with a sip of wine. "Really good. Word has it

Whitestone and Louret are considering her for their next promotions, too."

Louret. Trace refrained—barely—from curling a lip, told himself it didn't matter one bit if his estranged family hired Becca or not. "And you're telling me this because?"

"Thought you might like to know she'll probably be around for a while," Reed said with a shrug. "Just in case you want to, ah, catch up on old times."

"Nothing to catch up on." Reed was fishing and Trace had no intention of taking the bait. "Doesn't interest me in the slightest."

But it appeared that several people here at the party were interested, Trace thought irritably, noticing the whispered conversations after a few of the guests glanced his way. He should have sent Paige here today, dammit. He felt like he was under a damn microscope.

He wished to God that Becca had never come back to Napa. There'd been a growing aggravation in the pit of his stomach since she'd returned.

When another vintner pulled Reed away, Trace downed what was left of his wine. He thought about leaving, which only aggravated him all the more. Why the hell should he leave because Reed had mentioned Becca, or because a few busybodies couldn't mind their own business?

He wouldn't, dammit. Several of Ashton Estate Winery's accounts were here today, not to mention potential clients. Trace knew the value of schmoozing, it was part of his job. He was here to work, he reminded himself, and managed to spend the next fifteen minutes doing exactly that before he strolled up the stairs leading to the second floor where ceiling-high glass windows looked down on the barrel room twenty feet below. The well-lit room was the size of a high school gymnasium, with fifteen-feet cement aisles separating oak barrels stacked on their sides, seven high and three wide.

When Becca backed out from one of the aisles, Trace sucked in a breath.

She was deep in thought, her slender fingers idly stroking her chin, her lips pursed and eyes narrowed. She'd dressed for the cool temperatures in the room—hooded navy sweatshirt under a denim jacket, tan suede knee-high boots over jeans that hugged a well-rounded bottom.

The breath he'd been holding hissed out between his teeth. She had no damn right looking so damn sexy dressed as she was. No right at all.

She tilted her head one way, then the other, then

hunkered down, stretching those snug jeans over her bottom even tighter. When she leaned forward, her shirt rode up, exposing the small of her back.

Son of a bitch.

Lust rolled over his tongue, and when he swallowed, it burned like molten steel all the way down to his gut. It hurt just to breathe.

He hadn't felt a sexual pull of this intensity for five years. He hated her for that, hated that she had that kind of effect on him. Hated himself even more for wanting her.

He could walk away right now, go back to the luncheon, have another glass of wine, chitchat, then get the hell out. God knew that's what he *should* do.

Instead he turned, walked to the end of the landing, then opened the door leading into the barrel room, cursed himself with every step down the stairway. The familiar scent of oak filled the damp air and the hollow ring of silence surrounded him. Silence suddenly broken by soft singing. He stopped and listened, raised a brow when he caught the verse.

"…sixty-three bottles of Cabernet on the wall, sixty-three bottles of Cabernet, take one down, pass it around, sixty-two bottles of Cabernet on the wall…"

Not exactly how he'd remembered the song, but

he definitely remembered the silky voice. A voice that had turned his insides out when she'd whispered in his ear or sighed his name. A voice that had also lied and deceived him. Once again he thought about simply turning around and walking away. Once again, he moved forward.

He held back just as she stepped around a corner of stacked barrels, watched her adjust her light banks, then move to a black box sitting three feet away from the display she'd designed on an antique buffet table. Glossy blackberries flowed from a silver bowl, eucalyptus branches spilled from a woven basket, sprigs of mint swirled around the base of an empty goblet, all rushed together over a shimmering river of moss green satin. When she flipped a switch on the black box, an eerie, thin cloud of fog rolled across the table.

He could almost taste the blackberry and mint and eucalyptus on his tongue, could feel a sense of mystery in the swirling fog. She reached out and plucked a blackberry from the bowl, then popped it in her mouth. His throat went dry when she sucked on it.

Dammit, but this was a bad idea. He'd told himself that he'd come here for the luncheon, but looking at Becca, he realized exactly why he'd come here.

Because he'd known she'd be here.

Continuing to murmur her silly song, she stepped behind her camera and snapped pictures. She worked with focused intensity, as if nothing else in the world existed. She'd always been confident when she had a camera in her hands, he thought, remembering the first time he'd seen her. She'd come to the Ashton estate to take photos of the house and grounds for a local lifestyle magazine. He'd been assigned the boring task of tour guide.

But the day had turned out to be anything but boring. Her passion for her work, her enthusiasm, had been contagious. Rainbows of light streaming through beveled glass, a rusting weather vane, a bright blue dragonfly scooping water from a stone fountain. She'd captured all those things with her camera and made them look special.

That day, he'd seen the world he'd grown up in and taken for granted through Becca's eyes. It had never looked the same since.

She switched from counting bottles of Cabernet and started to sing about red, red wine. When her hips began to move in rhythm to the song, Trace gritted his teeth. As much as he wanted to be immune to this woman, he still had blood in his veins. And because that blood was suddenly pumping faster, he stepped away from the barrels and moved out into the aisle.

Before Becca even turned, she knew it was him.

The sound he'd made was no more than a slight scuff of a shoe on concrete, and still she'd known.

Her pulse skipped.

She shot several more pictures, then managed to pulled herself together before she straightened and faced him. "Trace, hi."

"Hi." He glanced at her camera. "Mind if I take a look?"

She hesitated, then shrugged and moved aside, shoved her hands into her pockets. "Sure."

Becca did her best not to fidget while he stared through her viewfinder. As cool as the room was, she felt perspiration dampen her underarms. It was only seconds, but it felt more like hours before he finally straightened and looked at her.

"You always had an eye for this."

Silly that his approval should mean so much to her after all these years. But strangely, she acknowledged, it did. "You take enough pictures, you're bound to get a few decent ones."

"You were always modest, too."

Though she doubted that Trace had intended his comment to be sexual, she couldn't stop the images flooding her mind. The first time he'd kissed her, the first time he'd unbuttoned her blouse and touched her. The first time they'd made love. She *had* been modest, but his rough hands on her skin, his hot mouth, had been so thrilling, so exciting, she'd forgotten her shyness.

Afraid that he would see the heat rushing into her cheeks, she moved to her display and turned off the smoke machine, then meticulously rearranged mint leaves, praying he wouldn't see her fingers were shaking. "So what brings you here?"

"Harvest tasting and luncheon." He wandered to a prop table, picked up one of several wine books stacked there.

"I believe the tasting is upstairs."

"I read this one." He flipped through the book in his hands. "Not bad, but I didn't agree with the author's opinion on *terroir*. I believe in micromanaging yield, ripening extraction and filtration undermine the effect."

"Trace." Swallowing the lump in her throat, Becca turned. "Why are you here?"

"Funny—" he closed the book and set it down, leveled his gaze with hers "—I've been asking myself the same question. Then it occurred to me."

Her pulse jumped when he moved toward her. "What occurred to you?"

He moved closer, so close she could feel the heat of his body, see the icy cold in his eyes. He placed his arms on either side of her and though she knew she should push him away, she'd lost the capacity to move. Like a trapped bird, her heart fluttered frantically in her throat.

"Five years ago."

Five years ago? His words formed in her brain, but she couldn't make sense of them, nor could she speak. His scent, so familiar, so masculine, enveloped her like a soft web. Though she wanted to lean into him, to wrap her fingers in his shirt and drag him closer, she reached behind her and tightly gripped the table's edge instead.

"Five years ago," he repeated, his voice quiet and husky. "You left me without even a kiss goodbye."

Even as he lowered his head to hers, she thought this couldn't be possible. She couldn't breathe, was completely incapable of resisting him, or even protesting.

"I think I at least deserve a kiss goodbye, Becca," he muttered, and dropped his mouth roughly on hers.

A lightning bolt of emotions exploded inside her. Shock, excitement. *Pleasure.* Even after five years, even knowing that he must hate her, she couldn't stop the reaction spiraling from her toes upward.

There was nothing gentle about his kiss, nothing tender, but that didn't seem to matter. She was burning up, her skin, her bones, melting under the crush of his mouth against hers.

Desperate to keep her control, she grabbed hold of the table even tighter, fought back the overwhelming need to wrap her arms around his neck, to pull him closer, to return his kiss. His tongue, hot and demanding, plunged between her lips. Everything inside her, every swirling thought, every sensation, every cell, burst into flames.

He yanked his mouth away, then stepped back. She heard the sound of his breathing, felt the rise and fall of her chest and the slam of her heart against her ribs. Slowly she opened her eyes and met his hard gaze.

"Goodbye, Becca," he said tightly, then turned and left.

Several moments passed before she could move. *I deserved that*, she thought, her heart aching. When she finally found her legs, she turned, then dropped her head into her hands and waited for the trembling to stop.

Three

3:14 a.m.

Trace stared at the illuminated readout on his bedside clock. For the past two hours, each soundless, endless minute had crashed into the next, bathing the darkness in its mocking red glow.

Teeth gritted, he flipped to his side and shut his eyes, felt the numbers burn into his back. Into his brain.

3:15

He seriously considered heaving the clock against the wall, but knew that the satisfaction would not only be fleeting, it would prove what he already knew.

He was a damn fool.

In an unexplainable brain lapse, he'd given in to an unreasonable and illogical Neanderthal need to prove to Becca that he was indifferent to her. That he could touch her, hold her, kiss her, then just walk away without feeling a damn thing.

He could still taste her, dammit. Blackberries, sweet and plump and juicy. Her lips had been as soft as he'd remembered, and though she hadn't kissed him back, he'd heard the catch in her throat, felt her shiver of response, and he knew she hadn't been immune to the desire.

From the first day he'd met her, the chemistry between them had always been potent. Obviously it didn't matter that he no longer loved her, or that she didn't love him. The attraction was still there. Just as heady, just as powerful.

3:16

Sexual frustration coiled in his body like a steel cable, cinching tighter and tighter, until the aching need in his groin had him kicking off the covers and dragging on a pair of sweatpants. What the hell, he wasn't getting any sleep tonight, anyway. He might as well get up and do something productive. He'd be damned if he'd spend the next three hours tossing and turning, counting each and every minute, kicking himself because he'd kissed Becca.

He flipped on the light in the living room of his apartment in the west wing of his family's estate. The glossy hardwood floors were cool and smooth under his bare feet, and the faint scent of orange wax lingered from the housekeeper's earlier cleaning. Scrubbing a hand over the early morning stubble on his face, Trace poured himself a shot of Glenlivet he kept in the bar, tossed it back, then poured himself another shot and opened the French doors leading onto the second-floor balcony. The night was clear and cold and the icy air felt good on his bare chest, sucked the last vestiges of sleep from his brain and cooled the heat of lust still pumping through his veins.

It wasn't as if he'd been celibate for the past five years. He might not have dated anyone seriously, but he'd managed to satisfy the basic needs of a healthy man. It had been a while, though, he realized. Maybe that was his problem. Maybe he just needed a night of hot, sweaty, no-holds-barred sex.

A couple of women came to mind. Jennifer, that cute, curvy blonde who worked the reception desk at the gym had slipped her phone number to him last week. And Charlotte, the restaurant manager with the long legs and big blue eyes was a possibility. He'd met the pretty brunette on his last sales trip to San Francisco. She'd made it clear she was looking for some fun without the hassle of a relationship.

Jennifer or Charlotte?

Why not both? He raised a brow at the idea, then shook his head.

Oh, hell, who did he think he was kidding?

Frowning, he stared at the glass in his hand. Not two, not even two hundred women would appease the gnawing ache in his gut.

Only one woman could.

As much as he hated to even consider the possibility, maybe his sister was right. Maybe he did need some kind of closure with Becca. There might not be anything emotional between them anymore, but last night had proven that the physical attraction was still there.

And not just on his part, either.

He'd been caught off guard when she'd walked out on him five years ago, chosen a career and money over being his wife. At the time, it had been difficult to know who he'd hated the most, his father for paying her off or Becca for accepting the check. He'd nearly gone to Italy and tracked her down to confront her, to make her look him straight in the eyes and tell him to his face that she didn't love him.

But the canceled check his father had shown him had spoke louder than any words could, and his pride had refused to allow him to make a bigger fool out of himself then he already had.

Light from a half moon cast long shadows over the vineyard that stretched out across the rolling landscape. As far as the eye could see—row after row of winter-bare vines. All of it, the land, the estate, millions of dollars, was one-fourth his now. If Becca had loved him enough to stay, they would have shared it together.

But she hadn't.

He downed the rest of his drink and rolled the glass in his hand. He'd do whatever he needed to do to get Becca in his bed one last time, he decided, and then he'd have her out of his system for good.

Closure.

Why the hell not?

* * *

Becca took a long, hot shower in the morning, prayed that the blast of nearly scalding water would stop the shivering that seemed to radiate from deep inside her bones. She figured if she could get her blood pumping, she just might be able to survive the day on less than four hours sleep.

Closing her eyes, she turned her back to the pulsing spray and sucked in a breath. It was much easier to take the pain of the pounding needles than the pain of reliving Trace's kiss.

The taste of his anger had lingered on her lips all night.

She knew she should be repelled, disgusted even, by such a blatant display of rude, macho intimidation. But to her shame and humiliation, she wasn't.

Her lips still tingled, her pulse still raced, her breasts ached. The harder she tried not to think about it, the more intense the sensations became. The snippets of sleep she'd managed had been filled with erotic dreams. Trace kneeling on the bed beside her, reaching out to her, pulling her body against his. Hot, bare skin against hot, bare skin. His mouth, his tongue, working his magic down her neck, her breasts, her stomach. And every time, when he would slide into her, she'd wake, gasping, his name on her lips, her heart pounding fiercely, her body shaking with need.

It had felt so real. So incredibly, wonderfully real.

Somehow she'd managed to shut away those feelings for the past five years—how else would she have survived? Seeing Trace again had blown open and laid bare every emotion she'd buried and denied. Seeing Trace had left her exposed and raw.

With something between a sigh and a moan, she laid her forehead against the cool tile, wasn't certain she could bear to face him again.

Wasn't certain she could bear not to.

She toweled off, dragged a brush through her hair, then frowned at the dark circles under her eyes. *Nothing a can of wall putty can't fix,* she thought miserably. Still, she did her best with a tube of cover-up and a light brush of mascara, then pulled a teal-blue sweater over her head, hoping some color would brighten her pale cheeks.

Knowing her mother had come in late again, Becca crept down the hall, doing her best to avoid the creaks in the floor. She grabbed her purse off the kitchen counter and rummaged for her car keys while she quietly let herself out the front door.

When a movement from the end of the porch startled her, she dropped her keys.

Trace!

Hands in the pockets of his black leather jacket, he'd propped himself against the porch rail and casually stretched his long legs out in front of him. A fine layer of mud covered his work boots and the bottom of his worn jeans. For one crazy moment, it was five years ago. He'd come from an early morning in the vineyards; she was on her way to her class at Napa Valley College. For those few stolen minutes, nothing else, and no one else in the world had existed but the two of them.

She blinked and the moment was gone. She watched him straighten, then nod at her. "Morning, Becca."

Morning, Becca? Yesterday it had been *Goodbye, Becca,* after he'd kissed her and turned her world upside down. Now he had the nerve to stand on her front porch as if he belonged there and simply say *Morning, Becca*?

He moved toward her. "I would have knocked, but I figured your mom was sleeping."

Maybe it was the lack of sleep that suddenly made her cranky. Maybe she'd finally come to her senses. But she refused to show weakness. Refused to let him see that what had happened between them the day before had nearly brought her to her knees.

She knelt to pick up her keys, but he scooped them before she could reach them.

Pressing her lips firmly together, she frowned at him. “What are you doing here, Trace?”

At the sound of a diesel engine starting, Trace glanced across the street, watched a white pickup back out of the driveway. He waited until the truck drove away, then said, “I was out of line yesterday.”

An apology? That would be the last thing she’d expect from him. Once again he’d caught her off guard. “It doesn’t matter.”

“Yeah, it does.”

He handed her the keys, lightly brushing her palm with his fingertips. Tiny currents of electricity shot straight up her arm. When she started to pull her hand away, he closed his fingers around hers.

“But the thing is,” he said, meeting her gaze, “I’m not sorry.”

If he was trying to mess with her mind, he was doing a hell of a job. She couldn’t get her balance with him, couldn’t think straight. Closing her eyes, she took in a slow breath. “Trace—”

“What I mean is,” he said, his voice low and rough, “I’m not sorry I kissed you.”

She opened her eyes, tried to read his expression, but couldn’t. “Why are you doing this?” she whispered.

He traced his thumb over her knuckles. "It was always good between us."

She blushed at the sexual connotation in his voice, and though she should be offended by it, it was a statement of fact. It *had* been good. More like spectacular. "That was a long time ago."

"Some things don't change, Becca."

"Everything changes," she said quietly.

"Sometimes they get better." His thumb continued its path over her little finger. "Tell me you didn't feel anything yesterday."

"I didn't feel anything yesterday." She swallowed the lie along with the dryness in her throat and pulled her hand away.

"Okay," he said with a nod that implied he didn't believe her but he'd let it go. "Have dinner with me tonight. We'll catch up on old times."

Old times?

She noticed he hadn't shaved this morning, remembered what that rough stubble felt like on her fingertips, against her cheek, and just the memory of it made her pulse quicken.

The *last* thing she wanted to do was catch up on old times. "I don't think that's a good idea, Trace."

"Which?" he asked. "Dinner, or catching up?"

Neither. "I—I can't."

His eyes narrowed slightly. "Are you seeing someone?"

Desperately she wanted to lie, knew it would be easier for her if she did. But there'd already been too many lies between them. She dropped her gaze and shook her head.

"It's just dinner, Becca." He reached out and traced a finger along her jaw, then lifted her chin. "What are you afraid of?"

You, she wanted to say. He made her want something she knew she could never have. They may have both changed, but the reasons they could never be happy together hadn't changed. As wonderfully tempting as it would be to fall back into Trace's arms and his bed, she didn't think her heart could survive leaving him again if she did.

Just dinner? They both knew better.

"I have to go to work," she said softly.

"All right." Dropping his hand, he nodded slowly. "See you around."

She watched him walk toward the black SUV he'd parked on the street. "Trace."

He stopped and glanced at her over his shoulder.

"I really think it's best if we don't see each other again."

He stared at her for a moment, then, slowly, one

corner of his mouth tipped upward. Without a word he turned and got in his car, then drove away.

When his car was out of sight, Becca slowly released the breath she'd been holding. There'd been no mistaking the challenge in his eyes and the purpose in his stride. His intentions were perfectly clear.

She just needed to keep her mind on her work, get through the next few weeks and avoid him, she told herself. If she could do that, then she would be home free.

Four

"The soil results on the east lot section are on the top file and the fermentation reports are ready." Greta, Trace's office manager, set a thick stack of folders on his desk. "And the president of Napa Valley Vintueis wants to know if you can come to a meeting Wednesday night."

Greta, a mother of five and grandmother of three, had been with the Ashton Estate Winery for eight years. She was a no-nonsense woman with a sturdy build, short blond hair and intense blue eyes that never missed a thing—a trait that could either be a blessing or a curse, depending on the situation.

"What for?" Trace didn't even glance up from the sales graph he'd been studying on his computer monitor. Because of an early spring this past year and warm, consistent weather, the early harvest had yielded one of the highest quality years ever. Production and sales were up a whopping eight percent.

"Environmental."

Damn. Those meetings always went on forever. Not that he wasn't all for the environment, of course. Maybe he could send Paige. "I thought I was scheduled for some kind of a silent auction Wednesday."

Greta pointed at his desk calendar. "That's next Wednesday. And it's a cocktail party and silent auction for the Childstart Literacy program."

"So when's the Rotary Club tasting?" he asked absently, knowing it was sometime soon.

Greta sighed with exasperation and flipped open the day planner on the desk. "This Thursday. And in case you've forgotten, Sunday night is your mother's birthday dinner at Le Sanglier."

"I haven't forgotten." Trace noticed a slight spike in bottling costs and made a mental note to check with the supplier. "So what did I buy her?"

"A scarf." Greta pulled a credit card receipt from the clipboard in her hand and set it on the desk.

"Thanks." Trace glanced at the receipt and lifted a brow. "For a scarf?"

"Italian cashmere and silk," Greta said evenly. "Your mother's having a difficult enough time accepting her upcoming role of grandmother. A birthday, this one especially, makes it even harder."

"And a little scrap of silk is going to make her feel better?"

"Absolutely. The color is perfect for her hair color and skin." At the sound of her phone ringing from the outside desk, Greta turned. "And besides, it's Hermes. Even if she hated it, she'd love it."

At that price, he certainly hoped so, Trace thought when Greta closed the door behind her. Heck, he could probably pay for her airfare to go to Italy and buy all the silk she wanted for that amount.

Women.

He wasn't going to pretend he even remotely understood the female gender. The only thing he'd learned about women was that he knew nothing at all about them. What they thought, what they wanted.

If they ever said what they really meant.

I don't think we should see each other again.

With a sigh, he leaned his head back and closed his eyes. He'd given Becca's statement a lot of thought over the past two days. He'd almost believed that she'd meant it, but something in her eyes, as subtle as it was fleeting, had denied her words.

They'd see each other again, all right. He intended to make certain they did.

What he couldn't figure out was why she was trying so hard to pretend she wasn't interested. And why, if she truly *was* indifferent, did she appear so flustered every time she saw him?

Maybe he'd misinterpreted her reaction. Perhaps it was pure and simple guilt that made her nervous—having to face the man she'd promised to love and marry, knowing she'd lied and accepted money to break that promise.

He clenched his jaw. What the hell difference did it make *what* she was feeling? Once he got her in his bed and out of his system, he wouldn't have to think about Becca Marshall ever again.

"Trace!"

A single swearword shot out of his mouth. He snapped forward in his chair so abruptly, he nearly fell out. Arms folded, Paige stared at him from the other side of his desk.

"What the hell are you doing?" he growled.

"What am *I* doing?" She rolled her eyes. "I not only knocked, I said your name twice."

His heart was still thumping against his rib cage.

"Can't I close my eyes for a minute without getting the bejesus scared out of me?"

"My, my." Paige lifted one thin brow. "Aren't we touchy today?"

"I am *not* touchy."

"Yes, you are. And you were touchy yesterday, too."

"I was not, dammit."

"Yes, you were," Greta called from the outside office.

"See?" Paige flopped down in an armchair. "So what gives?"

"Nothing gives." Grinding his teeth, Trace got up and slammed the door shut. "I take it you came by for a reason other than to annoy me?"

"Not really."

Like hell, he thought. It was written all over her face. "What do you want, Paige?"

"What every woman wants," she said longingly. "Romance, chocolate, world peace. Not necessarily in that order."

He crossed his arms and glared at her. "Some of us are working here."

"You were sleeping," she pointed out.

"Paige," he warned.

"All right, all right." She smiled sweetly. "I'm going to see Jack and I want you to come with me."

Good Lord, but the woman had a one-track mind. “I’m busy, Paige.”

“Those stats aren’t going anywhere in the next hour,” she said, glancing at his computer monitor.

“Neither am I, dear sister.” Trace turned his attention back to his work. “Neither am I.”

“All right, fine.” Paige rose on a sigh. “Have it your way. I just hope that this time you don’t wait until it’s too late.”

Trace stared at the doorway after Paige left. What the hell did she mean by that? Frowning, he shook his head.

Women.

Becca stared out of the sliding-glass doors that overlooked the Louret Winery vineyards. Row after endless row of vines marched neatly across the land. It didn’t matter that the branches were bare and lifeless at this time of year; the magnificence of its stark splendor had always stirred something in her.

She remembered the first time Trace had given her a tour of the Ashton Estate vineyards. She’d loved the rugged scent of the soil, the earthy colors and textures of the landscape, the excitement of harvest. She hadn’t just fallen in love with Trace that day, she’d fallen in love with the land, as well.

It would be so much easier if she had never met him. She wouldn't have to compare every other man she'd attempted to date since she'd left Napa, wouldn't have to find them all lacking. It would only be more difficult now that she'd seen him again.

Now that he'd kissed her.

She tried to tell herself she was relieved she hadn't seen or heard from him since the morning on her front porch, but if she were to be honest, there was a tiny part of her that was disappointed. A foolish, tiny part of her that searched for him while she was driving through town or picking up groceries or stopping at the bank. A part of her that had wished she'd said yes when he'd asked her to dinner.

That part of her that she continually told to be quiet.

"Sorry to keep you waiting, Miss Marshall."

Becca turned at the greeting and watched Mercedes Ashton-Maxwell step into the covered lanai. Soft, light brown curls fell over the woman's slender shoulders. A simple black skirt skimmed her knees, and a pale yellow V-necked cable-knit sweater covered her very pregnant belly.

Trace's half-sister.

Becca swallowed the sudden dryness in her throat and smiled. "Please. Just Becca."

"Mercedes."

Like Trace, Mercedes's eyes were deep green, though not quite as intense. And like Trace, she carried herself with the same composed confidence and cool reserve.

"Thank you so much for coming to the Vines." Mercedes gestured to a wicker sofa. "I appreciate you meeting with me here instead of town."

"It's no problem at all," Becca said. "Your home is beautiful."

In fact, it was stunning. Though not as large as the Ashton Estate, the French-country charm of The Vines was warm and friendly, the house filled with color and bright rooms.

The compliment brought a smile to Mercedes. "We like it, though my husband and I have our own place now. Can I get you something to drink? Some coffee or soda?"

"I'm fine, thank you."

"It's such a pleasure to finally meet you," Mercedes said. "You know there's been quite a buzz about you in Napa."

"A buzz?" Becca frowned. "About me?"

"I don't have to tell you our Valley is a close-knit community, Becca. The vintners even more so. Ivy Glen is raving about your work."

"They are?" The words slipped out and Becca blushed. *Way to go*, she thought. So much for presenting the image of a confident businesswoman.

Mercedes laughed. "And you're modest, too. I like that. So tell me, how much do you know about Louret Vineyards?"

At least this was something she felt confident about. Because it was important for a client to know she had an understanding of their business, Becca always meticulously researched a company before an interview. "Your mother started the winery twenty-five years ago. You have sixty-five acres of vineyards and produce about twenty thousand cases annually, mostly red estate wines. Your Cabernet is award-winning and your Chardonnay is also gaining great reviews. For the last three years you've been named the best boutique winery in Napa."

"You've done your homework." Mercedes nodded approvingly. "My mom and dad have pretty much retired, though. My sister and brothers and I are running Louret now."

Becca knew that, as well, including what each sibling's duties were in the business. Cole was the manager, Eli in charge of wine making, Jillian, research and development and Mercedes was in charge of marketing and promotion.

Mercedes sucked in a sharp breath and dropped both hands to her stomach. “Must be time for kick boxing practice.”

“Are you all right?” Worry pulled Becca out of her chair. “Should I call someone?”

Mercedes exhaled slowly. “I’m fine. Those little feet just catch me off guard sometimes.”

“Are you sure?” Becca bit her lip. “Maybe your husband, or your mother?”

Smiling, Mercedes shook her head. “I promise I won’t go into labor on you. You can sit back down.”

Cautiously, Becca eased back into the chair. “It’s no problem to reschedule.”

“Really, I’m fine.” Smoothing a hand over her stomach, Mercedes leaned back, seemed intent for a long moment, as if contemplating very carefully what she was about to say. “May I ask you something personal?”

The question was like her own little kick in the stomach. Becca resisted the urge to squirm. “Okay.”

“It’s about Trace.”

“Trace?” Becca’s fingers tightened on the portfolio sitting on her lap. “What about him?”

“I understand you were engaged to him.”

“I—” She had to clear her throat. “I was.”

“Obviously you know that he’s my half-brother.”

Even if she hadn't been engaged to Trace, Becca would have known that. Everyone who lived in the Valley knew that Spencer Ashton had abandoned his wife Caroline and their four children to marry his secretary, then had three children with her. "Yes."

"So you also know that our families have always been estranged, and since Spencer's death seven months ago, we've been in a legal battle over the estate."

It was more of a statement than a question, so Becca didn't bother to answer.

"It's not really about the money, you know. Personally, I wouldn't take one red cent." Mercedes sighed. "But the Ashton men have a lot of pride. Trace and Eli seem to have an extra dose. Those two can't get within ten yards of each other before they start swinging their fists. I can see I'm making you uncomfortable, Becca. I apologize."

"I just don't understand why you're telling me this," Becca said quietly.

"If we're going to be working together, I want to be sure it won't be difficult for you. That you won't feel you're in the middle of my family's problems, or you have to take sides. I personally hold no ill will for Trace, and I'm hoping that somehow we'll all be able resolve our differences."

"Trace and I broke up five years ago." It was so strange, discussing Trace with Mercedes. Strange and definitely unsettling. "I'm sorry if your family is having problems, but it's absolutely none of my business. I assure you, my past relationship with your brother will in no way affect my work."

"I'm the one who's sorry, Becca." Mercedes reached out and touched Becca's hand. "I didn't mean to embarrass or offend you."

"You didn't, I'm not." But her heart was still fluttering in her throat. "It's fine."

"Well, then." Smiling, Mercedes dropped her hand and glanced down at the portfolio in Becca's lap. "Now that we've got that out of the way, why don't you show me your work."

Five

Bodies of every shape and size packed the Saturday night grand opening of Elaine's Pub and Pool. Blue collar, white collar, young and old, single and married, all seemed to be enjoying the evening festivities, which included free T-shirt giveaways every hour. Animated conversations mixed with an enthusiastic deejay spinning records, the clack of pool balls and a fiercely competitive game of darts that had induced a rowdy burst of laughter and cheers.

Becca was amazed, and impressed, at the extent of the changes her mother had made in the business since she'd taken over. Fresh paint on the walls, new overhead lighting, improved ventilation system for the smoke and a nonsmoking area, too. She'd even added a creative menu of appetizers that included "Hit Man Chicken Wings," so dubbed because they were killer, and "Dragon Puffs," spicy cheese-stuffed jalapeños so good they could make a grown man cry.

The weekend deejay had also proved to be a big hit, Becca noted, and a well-rounded selection of music kept the small dance floor crowded. Currently, a lively disco-reggae rendition of "White Christmas" was pumping the room.

"Three Buds, a Heineken, and two Cokes," Becca shouted to Candy, one of the three part-time bartenders who'd just been hired. The young woman, with her cropped blond hair and big blue eyes, was already popular with the clientele, not only because she was pretty, but because of her theatrics. Candy could sing country music, juggle bottles of alcohol and she made a fantastic margarita, as well.

The fact that she filled out the Elaine's Pub T-shirt quite well didn't hurt, either.

Becca glanced down at her own T-shirt. If this was her livelihood and she had to rely on tips based on bra size, she knew she'd be in big financial trouble.

"Becca," her mother called from a nearby table

where she'd been mingling with several customers. "Take a break after you deliver that order, honey. You've been on your feet for more than three hours."

Her mom looked beautiful tonight, Becca thought. Her smile was radiant, her eyes shone with laughter. There'd been so many rough times, so many years that they'd barely managed to get through, and seeing her mother this happy made Becca's throat tighten with love and pride.

She wondered sometimes if her mother was lonely, if she wished she had someone to share her life with. She dated sometimes, but as far as Becca knew, none of those men she'd gone out with had been anything more than casual friends or an occasional blind date. They never talked about it, but Becca had often wondered if her mother been so in love with Becca's father that no other man could take his place?

Becca couldn't help but wonder if her own life might end up the same as her mother's. If the love she'd known with Trace would make it impossible to ever truly care for someone again, to settle down and have babies and a real home.

She glanced at a man and woman sitting in a corner booth, watched the couple kiss, then exchange an intimate smile. An ache settled in her chest and she quickly looked away. Desperately, she wanted that, had always wanted that.

She *would* love again, dammit, she thought, lifting her chin. She *would* have children and a home. She had to believe that.

As soon as she got back to Los Angeles, she'd start dating more. She'd given Trace too much power over her, it was time she took it back. She'd have an open mind with men, she resolved, and even more important, an open heart.

With that decision made, she felt lighter, in control again. She delivered her tray of drinks, exchanged banter with a couple of the older college guys who'd been flirting with her all night, then was heading for the employee lounge when a man's hand reached out from the crowd and caught her arm.

"Sorry—" she turned with a smile "—I'm on—"

Her smile froze. *Trace.*

No, no, *no!*

Her heart leaped into her throat. She quickly looked around, was terrified that the music would suddenly stop, then everyone in the room would go quiet and every head would turn and stare.

When he brought his mouth close to her ear, a shiver ran through her.

"Can I talk to you?" he asked.

She lifted her eyes to his, felt the burn of his dark green gaze. For one crazy moment, everything surrounding her faded away. The people, the music, even her mother. The past five years. For just that moment, she wanted to lean into him, to slip her arms around his neck and kiss him hello. For just one moment, she wanted to belong to him.

So much for taking back her power.

Just as quickly, reality came crashing back. "I'm working, Trace."

"Just give me a minute," he said firmly, sliding his thumb over the inside of her elbow. She felt the tingle all the way down to her toes.

The last thing she wanted was for her mother to see her talking with Trace, and based on the determination in his eyes, he wasn't going to take no for an answer.

Darn it!

She nodded toward a door that led to a side parking lot, then pulled out of his grasp and walked away. She told Candy she was taking a break, casually slipped into her coat, wrapped a scarf around her neck and stepped outside into the brisk night air.

She didn't see him at first. With his black jacket

and dark shirt, he blended in with the shadows in the parking lot. But when he pushed away from the side of the building, she took in a slow breath to fortify herself. *You can do this,* she told herself firmly. *You can, you can, you can.*

"I've only got a minute." Shoving her hands into the pockets of her coat, she moved toward him. "We're pretty busy in there."

"Your mom's done a hell of a job." He glanced over his shoulder. "The deejay's a nice touch."

"Thanks." Would she ever be able to look at him and not hurt? she wondered. There were times when she couldn't remember why she'd left, times when she couldn't remember anything but what it felt like to be in his arms.

"I heard you got an assignment with Whitestone."

She nodded. "I'm doing a layout for them for *Wine News* and some photos for an Internet site."

He stepped closer to her, reached out and lifted one end of the scarf she'd wrapped around her neck. "Does that mean you'll be staying longer?"

Slow down, she told her pulse. It didn't listen. "Just a couple of days. You said you wanted to talk."

"I do." He lifted the other end of her scarf. "I'll pick you up in the morning. We can drive into Sausalito and have lunch at Pascale's."

Pascale's had been their favorite restaurant at the cozy little town outside of San Francisco. They'd spent hours there just walking on the wharf and watching the boats in the marina. The weekend he'd proposed, they'd stayed at a small bed-and-breakfast there and made love for hours. The memory made her breath quicken and her blood heat up.

"Trace, no." She resisted when he tugged on her scarf.

He held firm. "All right, let's make it dinner, then."

"No," she repeated, but even she knew there was no conviction in her voice.

"No to dinner?" he murmured, lowering his head. "Or no to this?"

He didn't wait for her to answer, just dropped his mouth over hers.

She wouldn't kiss him back, she told herself. Like the last time, if she could resist him, if she could prove she was immune and he had no effect on her, she was certain he wouldn't persist in this game of his.

But when the night closed around them like black velvet, when she breathed in the masculine scent that was his alone, when his tongue lightly traced the seam of her closed lips, every wall, every resolve, every thread of resistance dissolved like smoke in the wind.

Just one kiss, her mind whispered, then went blank.

On a soft moan her lips parted, her eyes drifted closed.

He took his time, nibbled lightly at the corner of her mouth, gently tugged her bottom lip with his teeth. Strands of pleasure streaked through her, braiding and unbraiding, tightening and flowing.

She wasn't sure when her hands had slipped from her pockets, but her fingers were suddenly gripping the front of his shirt, closing tightly around fabric. She was certain if she didn't hold on, her knees would give out completely.

When his tongue slipped inside, she thought she might cry from the sheer need that jolted her system. Dazed, she clung to him, heard that little voice that told her she would regret this later. But at the moment, she didn't care. She could only feel.

She met the hot thrust of his tongue with her own, shuddered at the sensations ripping through her. Her skin tightened, her breasts ached, she could feel her bones melting.

And the need, the throbbing need, centered painfully between her legs.

When he pulled away, she nearly whimpered in complaint.

"Becca," Trace whispered, his voice husky and strained. "I want you."

I know. I want you, too.

"Come home with me tonight," he said, brushing his lips over hers. "Stay with me."

How easy it would be to say yes. To be in his arms, in his bed, for even a few hours. Because she knew what they'd shared before, and knew instinctively that the time and distance between them would only make it better now, she nearly said yes.

Headlights from an approaching car flickered across the parking lot, reminding her where they were. Who she was, and who Trace was.

She wasn't strong enough five years ago and she wasn't strong enough now.

When he reached out for her, she shook her head and stepped back, watched his jaw tighten and the sharp planes of his face harden.

"Becca—"

"I've got to get back inside, Trace."

His hand dropped to his side and he nodded stiffly. "Tell your mom I said congratulations."

"Sure."

But they both knew she wouldn't. She turned and

slowly walked inside, closed the door behind her, then prayed desperately that somewhere she could manage to dredge up enough of a smile to help get her through the night.

Dammit, he was late.

Birthday present tucked under his arm, Trace followed the tuxedo-clad maître d' through the elegant dining room of Le Sanglier. Candles flickered on pink-linen-clad tables set with formal china, gleaming silver and sparkling crystal. Teams of waiters in crisp white shirts and black bow ties busily served meals from carts sizzling with thick, buttery steaks and flaming *crêpes suzette.* Instrumental holiday music drifted quietly amid the hushed conversations of couples out for an evening of fine French cuisine.

The restaurant, one of the top rated in Napa Valley, had recently been named Most Romantic Dining by Howard Bomgarten, a popular California food and wine critic. Paige had made the reservations four weeks ago for their mother's fiftieth birthday party, a birthday Lilah Ashton was less than enthusiastic about. And though she was reluctantly willing to accept the family party, she'd already made it clear that no one was allowed to mention the number.

He wouldn't have been late if he hadn't been

thinking about Becca again, Trace thought irritably. One minute he'd been studying a fermentation report and the next he was replaying—for at the least the tenth time—last night's encounter in the parking lot.

The woman frustrated the hell out of him. That kiss had proven she wasn't as indifferent—or disinterested—in him as she'd tried to make him believe. He'd heard her soft moan, felt her tremble under his touch. Dammit, she'd wanted him just as badly as he'd wanted her. She knew how good it had been between them. How good it could be again.

He just had to figure out a way to convince her.

At the sound of someone calling his name, Trace snapped out of his wayward thoughts, then looked up and saw another vintner waving hello. Trace waved back, then cursed himself, determined to push Becca out of his mind—for the evening, at least.

With a sigh, he glanced at his watch, knew his mother would be in a snit that he was ten minutes late. Her modus operandi would be a chilly greeting, then she'd ignore him for several minutes until she felt he'd been properly chastised.

"Right this way, Mr. Ashton." The maître d' glanced over his shoulder as he led Trace to a private room behind the main dining area, then opened the set of French doors and stepped aside. "May I take your coat, sir?"

Trace brushed away the light mist of rain that had fallen on his shoulders, then shrugged out of his coat and handed it to the man. “Thank you.”

“Ah, here’s the prodigal son now,” Paige said when Trace stepped into the room.

“Sorry I’m late.” Trace moved to his mother and gave her a perfunctory kiss on the cheek, then set her present on the table. “Happy birthday, Mom.”

“Thank you, dear.” Lilah patted his cheek and smiled cheerfully. “It’s no problem. We were just enjoying an aperitif.”

Trace exchanged a curious glance with his sisters, who both appeared as stunned as he was by their mother’s warm reception.

Who is this woman? he wondered. *And what has she done with my mother?*

She *looked* like the same woman, he thought. Chin-length red hair, lake-blue eyes that matched her Versace silk suit, nails and makeup impeccable. Lilah Ashton, all right.

It was hard to believe turning fifty had prompted such a sudden change. He loved his mom, but she’d always been overly dramatic, not to mention demanding. Her demeanor tonight was softer somehow, calmer. Lighter. She had a glow to her cheeks and an almost schoolgirl brightness about her.

Must be one of those fancy spa treatments she always went for, he thought. Whatever it was, he decided he liked it.

"Hey, Waddle." He moved beside Megan and placed a hand on his sister's very pregnant belly. "Aren't you about done in there?"

"I'm quite done," Megan replied testily, and tossed a lock of blond hair from her cheek. "In fact, I'm more than done. My daughter, however, is not."

"Don't get her going." Simon, Megan's husband, sent Trace an imploring look. "The doctor told her this morning that she probably won't deliver until after the first of the year and she's blaming it on me. Says our daughter has inherited my stubborn gene."

"I'm sure that's true," Paige said, lifting a glass of water. "Everyone in my family has the patience of Job."

Matt, Paige's fiancé, rolled his eyes. "I suppose that's why I saw you shaking your Christmas present yesterday."

"I was just moving it," Paige insisted petulantly.

Trace chuckled then noticed their cousin Charlotte and her husband were missing. He knew that they'd been visiting Charlotte's mother in South Dakota, but they were supposed to have returned yesterday. "Where's Char and Alex?"

"A snow storm closed down the airport and delayed their flight," Lilah replied. "Charlotte called this morning to wish me a Happy Birthday. Walker and Tamra also sent their regards."

Walker have moved to South Dakota three months ago to get married and set up a new business. They'd had their differences in the past, and Trace was glad he and his cousin had made amends before he'd moved away.

Trace pulled out a chair to sit next to his mother. "How's his consulting firm doing in Sioux Falls?"

"Very well, Charlotte says. Dear, would you mind sitting over there?" Lilah nodded at an empty space between Megan and Paige. "I have a guest coming."

A guest? Trace glanced at Paige, who simply lifted a brow, then patted the chair next to her. What did she know that he didn't? he wondered.

"I'm so sorry I'm late, I hope you weren't waiting for me."

Trace turned at the sound of the man's familiar voice. Stephen Cassidy, the family's lawyer, stepped into the room. He had a small, gold-foil-wrapped box in one hand and a single red rose in the other.

Stephen was his mother's guest? Stephen, who'd been his father's personal lawyer for years? Stephen, who'd been handling not only the will, but all the Ashton legal issues, as well?

"Close your mouth, Trace," Paige whispered when he sat down beside her.

Trace glanced at his sister, who simply smiled and shrugged.

Apparently, at least one of his sister's had a clue what was going on here.

Dumbfounded, Trace watched a soft blush rise on his mother's cheeks when Stephen handed her the rose and birthday present. In his entire life, Trace couldn't remember seeing his mother blush—especially when his father had given her presents or flowers.

Stephen and his mother?

I'll be damned, he thought.

It wasn't that Trace had any objections to Stephen's obvious interest in his mother, or vice versa, he just felt a little silly that he'd been so completely clueless. Obviously he'd been even more preoccupied lately than he'd realized.

And anyway, they were certainly both adults, for God's sake. His mother was a beautiful woman; the debonair lawyer had been widowed himself for several years. Trace supposed it made sense. He watched them exchange a smile, saw the sparkle in their eyes.

They almost looked like teenagers, he thought, which only blew him away all the more. He didn't think he'd ever met two people more aloof and reserved and here they were, acting like a couple of kids.

The awkwardness passed after a toast of champagne and the opening of presents, and the dinner seemed strangely—well, normal. Stephen had been a part of their lives for practically as long as Trace could remember, so when the initial shock had worn off, the evening turned out to actually be pleasant. His mother didn't complain once, in fact, she'd been so wrapped up in hanging on Stephen's every word, she'd barely spoken herself at all.

It was obvious that his mother was just as taken with Stephen as the lawyer was with her, and while it was going to take some getting used to the idea, Trace decided he already liked the changes he'd seen in his mother's demeanor.

They were all having coffee and drinks after dinner when Trace excused himself and headed for the rest room. His mind was still on the budding romance when he spotted the woman he actually hadn't thought about for at least fifteen minutes.

Becca stepped through the front door of the restaurant, smiling as she tossed her hair back to shake off the rain. It occurred to him he hadn't seen that smile for five years, and he realized how much he'd missed it. He watched her slip her coat off and hand it to the maître d'—and felt as if he'd taken a fist straight to his gut.

Her short, black dress clung to every slender, feminine curve and dipped low enough in the front to bring a man's blood to a boil. Black stilettos made her heart-stopping, never-ending legs appear even longer.

He literally couldn't breathe.

He wasn't the only male in the room staring, Trace noted, glancing quickly around. Several men were openly gawking, much to their female companion's annoyance. Becca seemed oblivious to the attention as she spoke with the maître d'. Her eyelids were smoky-gray, her lips siren-red. A single string of tiny black glittering beads danced from each of her earlobes, lightly stroking the sides of her long, sleek neck.

She'd never known how beautiful she was, Trace thought, had always blushed when he'd told her and never really believed him. He'd always thought he'd have a lifetime to convince her.

Her gaze lifted then, almost as if she had read his thoughts, and her eyes widened when she saw him watching her. Even from across the room, he could see her cheeks turn red and her lips part with surprise.

He started toward her, froze when he saw Reed step into the restaurant and move toward Becca, then kiss her cheek. She turned and smiled at him, said something that made him laugh.

Reed? Everything inside Trace went numb. She was here with Reed?

What an idiot I am, he thought. Of course she was here with someone. Women didn't dress like that to go out by themselves or with a girlfriend. Numbness dissolved into anger and his hands clenched into fists when Reed slipped an arm around Becca's shoulders.

Dammit, anyway! It was bad enough he had to see her with another man, but to watch a friend touch Becca, to see him kiss her, was the final straw.

Hell, *any* man touching Becca would set his teeth on edge, he realized.

If he hadn't been so damned determined to get her in his bed any way he could, if he'd been thinking with his brain instead of another part of his anatomy, he wouldn't be standing here right now feeling like a complete fool. She might have kissed him last night and she might have wanted him, but his arrogance had obviously read more into it than was there.

His own plan had backfired on him, and as much as he'd like to punch Reed, he knew he had no one to blame but himself. Still, not quite certain what he might do if he saw his friend kiss Becca again, Trace turned abruptly and went back to his mother's party. He even managed to sing "Happy Birthday" and eat a slice of chocolate cake before finally leaving, made a point to keep his eyes straight ahead when he walked through the restaurant and out the front door.

The storm fit his mood, the accompanying lightning and thunder even more so. He was glad he'd driven his roadster tonight, and he headed for the highway, maneuvered through the icy sheets of rain faster than he knew he should and not giving a damn. The harder he tried not to think about Becca, the more she was there. In his mind, in his blood.

He white-knuckled the steering wheel, felt the need to get the hell out of Napa. San Francisco, he decided. He'd find a flea-bitten motel and drink himself blind. Even if only for the night, that would get the woman out of his mind.

A bolt of lightning speared the road ahead of him and the sky exploded with white. The roadster skidded sideways, then the back left bumper smashed into something and the car stopped. Swearing, Trace got out of his car and saw the Volkswagen-size boulder he'd struck.

That certainly made his night perfect.

Raking a hand through his drenched hair, he

climbed back into his car, knew that he should have been thankful that the air bag hadn't been deployed, but was too angry to care. When another crash of lightning struck close by and the ground shook with thunder, he started the car up again, winced at the sound of metal scraping against his fender when he pulled away from the boulder and got back on the highway.

He might be an idiot and a fool, but he wasn't completely stupid.

He headed back to his apartment, drove through the open wrought-iron gates and didn't even bother to park in the garage. He ignored the rain that pounded him as he walked up the outside stairs to his apartment, was contemplating a double Scotch when a dark figure standing on the landing brought him up short.

Adrenaline pumped through him, had him doubling his fists and bracing to charge. He almost enjoyed the idea of catching someone in the act of breaking in so he could smash their face.

And then lightning flashed and he saw who it was.

Six

"Becca! My God, what are you doing out here?"

The very question I've been asking myself, Becca thought.

With the rain pummeling down on her, she'd stood here on the landing for the past twenty minutes, arguing with herself, terrified that Trace would show up, terrified that he wouldn't. She wasn't certain if she was shaking from pure nerves or from the icy wind permeating her wet coat.

When she'd finally seen his car drive up, the knots in her stomach had twisted so tight she'd considered stepping back off the landing and hiding behind a potted tree. She might have, if she hadn't been too cold to move.

He didn't wait for her to answer him, he just rushed up the stairs, pulling his coat off and wrapping it around her shoulders while he dragged her to his front door. He dug his keys out of his pocket, dropped them, swore hotly and scooped them back up.

They were inside two seconds later. He slammed the door against the wind and rain, then disarmed the alarm and flipped on the light.

"What's wrong?" He spun around and grabbed her shoulders. His intense gaze quickly swept over her. Worry deeply etched his brow and tightened his jaw. "Are you hurt?"

She shook her head, heard the sound of her own teeth chattering.

"Come on." Taking her hand, he pulled her to the hallway.

"No!" She yanked her hand away, then slid his coat off her shoulders and handed it to him. "I can't. I—I'm all wet."

"Dammit, Becca—" he tossed the coat on the floor "—don't argue with me."

She gasped when he snatched her up in his arms and carried her. For one wild moment she actually thought he was taking her to his bedroom. Her heart leaped at the thought, and a mixture of excitement and panic filled her. But he took her into the small guest bathroom in the hallway, closed the toilet lid and carefully set her down there.

Opening a cupboard, he pulled out a stack of towels and set them on the brown-granite counter, then slipped her drenched coat off her shoulders and frowned at her. “How long were you out there?”

Shivering, she hugged her arms close to her, felt the rain sliding down her face and neck. Lord, she felt like a complete idiot. “Not very long.”

He draped one large, soft white towel over her shoulders, then grabbed another and blotted the water dripping from the ends of her hair. “You’re soaked to the bone.”

“I—I was just going to leave.” Not much of a response, she thought, but it seemed to be the best she could do under the circumstances.

Unable to stop the shaking in her hands, she gripped the ends of the towel around her shoulders and pulled it tighter. She was cold…so incredibly cold. His hands moved briskly over her back and shoulders. Warm, strong hands, she thought, remembering what those hands felt like on her bare skin. Tiny waves of electric current coursed through her, increasing her awareness of him, of his closeness. When his hands softened and slowed, she knew he felt it, too.

Kneeling beside her, he lifted her chin and gently wiped her forehead and cheeks. Too embarrassed to even look at him, she dropped her gaze.

"What in the world were you doing out there?" he asked quietly.

"Waiting for you."

He stilled; the words hovered between them for a few moments.

"I saw you at the restaurant," she said awkwardly, feeling more than a little foolish for stating the obvious.

"I saw you, too. In fact, I think every man in the room saw you." He set the towel down and lightly skimmed a finger along her cheek. "But that didn't answer my question."

She trembled at the gentle touch of his calloused fingertip on her skin. Her mind screamed at her to lie, to make up something—*anything*—so she could somehow leave here with at least a tiny piece of dignity.

No more lies, she told herself, and slowly raised her gaze to meet his. "You know why I'm here."

His eyes turned dark as a forest at midnight; his mouth pressed into a thin line. She felt the tension move from his body into hers, and like a living thing, coiled through her, tightening, burning.

"What about Reed?" he asked.

She closed her eyes, sucked in a fortifying breath. "It wasn't fair," she said softly. "Being with him, when I was thinking about you."

He tucked her wet hair behind her ears, then slowly slid his hands down her neck. "Open your eyes, Becca," he said hoarsely.

She did as he asked, felt her heart jump when she saw her own need reflected in his narrowed gaze. The intensity of her feelings frightened her. Slowly she raised a shaking hand and placed her fingertips on his warm cheek.

The anticipation of wanting a man—*this* man—of wanting him to make love to her, was almost more than she could bear.

She moved her fingers down his cheek, felt the light stubble of beard. Waves of pleasure skimmed through her. She touched his jaw, his chin, then moved upward to his lips, felt him stiffen under her touch. He took hold of her wrist.

"Trace," she whispered.

His name on her lips made his heart stop; the need in her soft brown eyes jump-started it again. The ache that had been slowly spreading through him took on a life of its own, became a living thing, a savage, primitive creature that had been denied for too long. But not tonight, he knew.

Not here, not now.

Her eyes shimmered with passion, her lips parted, waiting. He pulled her closer, breathed in the sweet scent of her, a mixture of rain and flowers and a scent that was hers alone.

His hands tangled in her wet hair and pulled her head back. Keeping his gaze locked with hers, he lowered his mouth. Her hands slid up his chest and her arms wound around his neck.

Their lips met, lightly at first, then suddenly he groaned and ground his mouth against hers, tasting her more deeply and intimately. She met the thrust of his tongue with her own, moving eagerly with the rhythm he set. She made a sound, a soft whimper of need, and he pulled away and stared down at her. Her cheeks were flushed with passion, her lips moist and swollen from his kiss.

God, she was beautiful.

She'd brought the storm in with her, he thought. It was here, in this room. In his body and his blood. Raging. Pounding. A fury that had waited five years to be released, and now that it was, could not, would not, be stopped.

You belong to me, he thought. If only for the moment, if only for the night, she was his.

"Kiss me, Trace," she breathed against his neck. "Kiss me, please."

She hadn't needed to ask twice. He felt the low, strangled moan deep in his throat as he caught her mouth with his. She clung to him, kissed him back with a passion that was so familiar. So right. Her soft breasts pressed against his chest, made his blood race and his heart pound. His hunger for her gripped him like a fist. He wanted to take her right here, in the hallway, on the floor, against the wall, anywhere, as long as he could bury himself deep inside her and ease the throbbing need in his groin.

Somehow he managed to make it to the bedroom. The light from the hallway washed across the bed. He reined his need in and lifted his head as he lowered her to the floor, sliding her body down his. When their bodies met intimately, her eyes widened and she looked up at him. There was no question what she'd done to him, or how badly he wanted her.

He saw the hesitation in her gaze, but he wouldn't ask her if she was sure. He didn't want her to think, dammit, didn't want to give her an opportunity to run from him again.

He caught her mouth with his, kissed her hard and long, until he felt her sway against him.

He reached for the zipper at the back of her dress and tugged it down, then slid his hands underneath the damp garment, slipped it off her shoulders.

It dropped to the floor.

He inched back, wanting, needing, to see her and his pulse stuttered at the exquisite sight. Her breasts, enclosed in black lace, were full and round, her skin smooth and creamy. A smile of black lace stretched across her slender hips and flat stomach. When he pressed his lips to her cool shoulder, he felt her shudder. She not only smelled like the rain, he thought, she tasted like it.

He heard her soft murmur asking him to hurry, but in spite of the need clawing at his gut, he simply had to touch her everywhere, had to reacquaint himself with every familiar inch of her.

Need coursed through Becca like a raging river. She bit her lip when Trace pressed his mouth to her stomach and she leaned into him, raking her hands through his thick, damp hair. When his hands covered her swollen, tight breasts, she sucked in a slow, deep breath. His fingers kneaded the tight buds of her nipples and pleasure, sharp and painful, ricocheted through her. He unhooked her bra and his mouth replaced his fingers as he tasted her.

Her world was spinning. No other man had ever made her feel this way, no other man ever could. Dread filled her at the thought, but she was lost and there was nothing she could do, nowhere she could go. Sensations pummeled her. His rough hands on her skin, his hot mouth on her breast, the hard ridge of his arousal pressing against her…

His mouth and tongue were hot and moist as they moved over her breasts and her stomach. When he slipped his fingers under the elastic band of lace at her hips and tugged them down, Becca felt the heat coil tightly between her legs. She stood naked in front of him, trembling not from the cold, but with need. Her fingernails curved into his shoulders.

He nuzzled her bra aside with his teeth and mouth, then clamped on her nipple. She moaned and arched into him.

They fell to the bed as one and rolled. She started with the top button of his shirt, slowly worked her way down to the waistband of his trousers before sliding her hands back up again over his flat, hard stomach and broad muscled chest. His body was like steel, strong and powerful. Rugged. The realization he was hers at last left her giddy and dizzy.

She pressed her lips to his chest, swept her tongue over his hot skin. The masculine, salty taste of him aroused her even more.

She forced her mind to concentrate on giving pleasure rather than receiving, but the two were intertwined. It was impossible to stop the fire racing in her blood. He squirmed when she slowly ran her fingertips over each rib bone, then across the hard muscles of his stomach. She unbuttoned his slacks with the intention of exploring her path to its final destination, but when she tugged his zipper down over the hard ridge of his manhood, he gave a low growl and suddenly it was she who was on her back. She barely had time to catch her breath before his shirt was off, his shoes, then his pants, until he stood gloriously and magnificently naked.

Her heart jumped at the sight of him, pounded furiously in her chest. He moved over her, slid his hands all the way up her legs to the top of her thighs, His lips followed the path of his fingers and he kissed the inside of each thigh, her knees, her calves, then back up again until she writhed frantically under him.

His mouth ascended her body, tasting the curve of her hip, the flat hollow of her stomach, the underside of her breast. She bit her bottom lip to keep from crying out, but when he covered the hardened peak of her nipple with his mouth, she did cry out, arching upward at the jolt of intense pleasure that surged through her. His tongue was hot and wet, he took her into his mouth and feasted hungrily on her. An ache spread through her body and centered between her legs, a pleasure that bordered on pain.

He moved to her other breast, gave equal attention there while he smoothed his palm over her hip, then her belly. His hand slipped between her legs, then slid between the sensitive folds there, stroking her gently at the same time he took her breast into his mouth.

It was more than she could stand. She moved urgently against him, raked his shoulders with her fingernails. "Trace, now, please!"

He needed no more encouragement. He spread her legs as he moved over her. His entry was hard and fast and she took him fully, lifting her hips to meet his. He made a sound, a deep animal-like noise, and moved inside her. She wound her legs tightly around him, wanting him closer still.

Lightning flashed, illuminating the room. Becca saw the fierce, wild expression on Trace's face as he moved deep inside her, felt his muscles bunch and ripple under her hands. An urgent, driving need consumed her. She wrapped her arms around his neck and surged upward, meeting every thrust of his body with her own.

The climax hit her like an explosion and she nearly screamed from the force of it. She shuddered over and over, and he lifted her hips higher still while he thrust wildly. On a low guttural groan, he shuddered, too, and she held on tightly while they rode the intense waves together.

When he collapsed on top of her, his breathing ragged, his heart pounding, she sighed and slid her arms around his neck.

It was a long while before either of them moved. Trace heard the sound of the rain, a hard, steady drum on the roof, but it seemed that the thunder and lightning had moved into the distance.

He was still trying to assimilate what had just happened, from seeing Becca with Reed at the restaurant, then at the top of his stairs, and now, in his bed. It all rushed together, and then there was only her, underneath him, naked.

The feel of her long, slender body under his gave him a primitive, physical sense of masculine satisfaction. He'd wanted her; he'd taken her. And the knowledge that she had wanted him, too, had only made it all the more powerful.

Because he didn't want to break the intimate contact between them yet, he shifted his weight and rose on his elbows, then stared down at her. The haze of desire still lingered in her eyes, but he also saw the confusion. The despair.

"I didn't want this to happen," she said softly.

Irritation flickered through him. Like hell she didn't. "You could have fooled me."

When she stiffened underneath him, he cursed his loose tongue, then sighed and lightly kissed her lips. "Regrets are for the morning, Becca. Save them until then."

She closed her eyes and nodded.

He felt the steady beat of her heart and the shallow rise and fall of her breathing. Her skin was warm and slightly damp from their lovemaking. And he was still afraid that he would wake up and realize he was dreaming. Or maybe he'd hit his head when he'd struck that boulder and none of this had really happened. He was still sitting in the front seat of his car on the highway, unconscious.

He brushed his lips over hers, then nibbled lightly at the corner of her mouth until he felt her relax again. She tasted real, he thought, and when she slid her hands up his back, he knew he wasn't dreaming.

"I should go," she said with a heavy sigh.

"You're staying the night." He moved to her ear, caught her lobe between his teeth.

She shook her head. "You know I can't."

"I know you can and you are." He felt her shiver when he slid his tongue over her ear.

"No—" she sucked in a breath when he moved down her neck "—my mom will worry if I don't come home."

And she'll want to know where you were, he thought. Or to be more precise, *who* she was with.

Once again, their past intruded. Once again, he pushed it aside. "You're a big girl, Becca. She won't worry if you call and leave a message you won't be home."

"No, I—"

"Yes." He trailed kisses over her collarbone, then moved lower, nuzzling the soft rise of her breast.

Biting her lip, she arched upward, then raked her fingers through his hair.

"Yes," she finally whispered, breathless, then sucked in a sharp breath when he moved lower. "Yes."

The dawn had barely broken when Trace woke. Sometime during the night the storm had moved on, and the only sound to break the morning stillness was the steady drip of water from the eaves outside his window.

A sense of deep contentment had settled heavily through his body. With great effort, he slid a hand over the warm sheets, found the space beside him cold and empty. Disappointment slammed into his chest.

For one brief moment he thought maybe last night hadn't happened. It wouldn't be the first time he'd dreamed about making love to Becca—though by far, it certainly felt as if it was the most real.

No, not a dream, he thought, breathing in her sweet scent. Thank God. She *had* been here last night, all right. In his bed, naked, as eager for him as he'd been for her.

So where was she now?

Frowning, he opened his eyes and looked around the room. No sign of her. When he saw that her clothes were missing, his frown darkened. Had she left?

Then the aroma of coffee drifted to him and, like a siren song, drew him out of bed. Slipping on a pair of jeans, he dragged a hand through his hair and headed for the kitchen.

His heart jolted at the sight of her standing at his kitchen sink, deep in thought as she stared out the window. Sleeves rolled to the elbows, she wore the pale blue dress shirt he'd had on last night. It skimmed her bare, creamy thighs and revealed long, sleek legs.

Because he needed a minute before he spoke—and because he needed something to steady himself—he leaned against the doorjamb and watched her.

Her hair, a wild mass of sandy-brown waves, swept over the soft curve of her shoulders. She'd always disliked the rain, he remembered, because it brought out the curl in her hair.

And yet, that's exactly where he'd found her last night. Standing in the rain. Waiting for him.

To think that he nearly hadn't come home at all, that he'd be in San Francisco right now if his car hadn't spun out and kissed that boulder. He certainly wouldn't have thought he'd be glad he'd crunched his bumper, but he was. For all he cared, he could have totaled the whole damn car as long as it brought him back here.

Last night, the only thing he'd cared about was making love to Becca. And as he stared at the woman standing in his kitchen, he realized that the only thing he cared about now was making love to her again.

He moved behind her and wrapped his arms

around her waist, then pulled her close. Knowing she was naked under his shirt made his blood heat. "My shirt never had it so good," he murmured.

A blush rose on her cheeks. "I put my damp clothes in your dryer. I hope that's all right."

"It's fine." He knew she was holding back from him. He could hear it in the formal tone of her voice, feel it in her body. Part of him wanted to know what she was thinking, but part of him didn't, was afraid she'd completely pull away if he asked.

"I made coffee, too," she said evenly. "I'll get you a cup."

When she started to move away, he tightened his arms around her. "Coffee can wait. I need to do this first."

He nuzzled her earlobe, then raked his hand upward through her hair to expose the back of her neck. He heard her soft intake of breath when he lowered his mouth and lightly nipped, felt her shiver in his arms.

He slid his hands under the cotton shirt, skimmed the curve of her hips and her bottom. Her skin was warm and soft, like rose petals, he thought. He could feel her pulse and breath quicken, matching his own. And when he moved upward to cup the round firmness of her breasts, she moaned and dropped her head back against his chest.

Gently he kneaded the soft flesh in his hands, felt her nipples tighten under his touch. She arched her back, pressing against him, and it felt as if every drop of blood in his body dropped below his waist. He lowered one hand between her legs and slipped a finger into the moist heat of her body, knew that she was as ready for him as he was for her. Kissing her neck, caressing her breast, he continued to stroke her, moving in and out. Gasping, she gripped his hips, then tried to turn. She cried out as the climax hit, and he felt the shudder move through her.

Turning her in his arms, he unzipped his jeans and shoved them down, then cupped her buttocks and lifted her. She wrapped her arms and legs around him and rose over him; he moaned when she slid down the length of him. He thrust hard and fast, groaning, then felt the insanity overtake him, too.

Her head resting on his broad chest, Becca lay in Trace's arms and waited for her senses to return. Through the haze of lingering passion, awareness of her surroundings slowly returned. The distant hum of a tractor, the bark of a dog. The steady beat of Trace's heart, the warmth of his bare skin against hers.

She'd lost all perception of time and place, wasn't

even certain how, or when, they'd ended up back in bed. She glanced at the bedside clock, was stunned when she realized it was nearly eight. It seemed that only minutes ago she'd been standing at the kitchen sink, preparing herself to face him, to be casual and completely comfortable with the fact that they'd just spent the night making love.

But then he'd touched her and once again her body had betrayed her.

Her date with Reed last night had been a disaster. She'd foolishly thought that accepting the man's invitation to dinner would help her forget about Trace, and though she'd done her best to be attentive, it hadn't taken Reed long to figure out that her mind wasn't on their meal or on him. It took him even less time to figure out who her mind *was* on.

And if that hadn't been embarrassing enough, it had been Reed who suggested they make an early night of it, then casually mentioned he'd seen Trace leave the restaurant.

Even as she was driving home, she told herself she wasn't going to Trace's. And then when she'd turned the car around, she told herself she would just talk to him for a minute, explain why it wasn't a good idea for them to see each other. The entire time she'd stood on his landing, she'd argued with herself to get out while she still could. She hadn't.

Last night he'd told her regrets were for the morning. But strangely, she had none. Even if she could, she wouldn't change what happened between them. No matter what happened now, she would cherish every moment.

"Where do you think you're going?" he asked when she started to pull away.

"To get my clothes." But she didn't resist when his arm tightened around her.

"I threw them away." His hand slid over her hip. "Why don't you put my shirt back on so I can take it off you again?"

"I seem to recall I was the one who took it off," she replied tartly.

"Okay, so now it's my turn."

She rose on one elbow and looked down at him, then quietly said, "You know I have to go."

With a sigh, he dropped his hand away. "I'll pick you up tonight at seven-thirty."

"Trace—"

"Just dinner." He reached out and brushed her hair away from her shoulder. "Morelli's still makes the best pepperoni pizza."

Sneaky bastard, she thought. He knew she could

never turn down a Morelli's pepperoni pizza. And after last night, how much harm could meeting him for a pizza do?

But still, she couldn't bring herself to say yes. Didn't know if she could trust herself to be close to him again.

"I'll try," was the best she could answer him, told herself that at least she'd have an option later if she came to her senses.

Too modest to walk across the room naked, she pulled on his shirt again, then glanced over her shoulder. The look in his eyes as he watched her told Becca she better get out of here quick or she'd crawl back between the sheets with him and do everything they'd already done all over again.

Seven

The twenty-two-thousand-square-foot Ashton Estate was built on the highest hill of the property's nearly two hundred acres. Sprawling exterior walls of cut, cream-colored stone, brick turrets and tall rock chimneys welcomed invited guests, and the luxurious interior of high ceilings, marble floors and spacious rooms impressed even the most sophisticated visitor.

To Lilah Ashton, who'd lovingly helped design and decorate the mansion, the house was everything. Until her husband's death, it had been the center of her social existence. Parties, fund-raisers, concerts—events at the Ashton estate were legendary, as well as memorable. Lilah had basked in the attention and respect her home had garnered.

But to Trace, the elegantly appointed rooms and gardens had always felt more like a museum than a home. He appreciated the beauty and the design, but as a place to live, the main house had always felt cold. For the most part, he'd preferred the stark simplicity of his room at boarding school to the aloof formality of Ashton Estate.

"I'm so glad you could join me for breakfast, dear." Lilah lifted the white china tea cup and delicately sipped her custom blend of cinnamon and orange pekoe. "I know what a busy schedule you have, but I just wanted to thank you again for last night."

Trace eyed his mother carefully over his coffee cup. He'd been out in the vineyard inspecting a new section of hybrid vines when she'd called and asked him to meet her on the veranda. His first thought was that she'd seen Becca leaving the estate this morning, but since his mother was not typically an early riser, he'd quickly rejected the idea.

Still, he knew that his mother had something on her mind other than thanking him for last night.

Sooner or later, she'd get around to the real reason she'd asked him here.

He just wished it would be sooner.

Lilah gestured toward a basket of assorted baked items. "Would you like a croissant?"

"I had one already, thanks." He'd also had bacon, eggs and potatoes. He hadn't realized how ravenous he'd been until he'd sat down and the cook had served him a plate. Apparently a night of making love with Becca had created one hell of an appetite.

And not just for food, either, he realized.

He couldn't wait to get his hands on her again, couldn't wait for her to be naked and moaning underneath him.

Realizing this was not exactly the best time to be thinking about Becca naked, Trace quickly forced the image out of his mind.

"Did I tell you how much I love the present you gave me?" Lilah asked, adjusting one corner of the blue scarf she'd skillfully knotted around her neck.

Several times, Trace thought, but decided not to call her on it. Clearly she was distracted this morning, and unless he missed his guess, she also appeared a little nervous. "I'm glad you like it, Mom."

"It was such a lovely party." Lilah's hand shook

slightly when she sipped her tea again. "It was very nice of Stephen to join us."

Ah.

So *that's* what this breakfast was really about. Stephen. If his thoughts hadn't been so consumed with the night he'd spent with Becca, he would have realized it much sooner.

"Very nice," he agreed, reaching for the carafe of coffee.

"Oh, let me do that, dear." Lilah poured the coffee, then anxiously adjusted the scarf around her neck again when he picked up his cup. "So what do you think?"

"Good coffee."

She frowned at him. "You know perfectly well what I mean."

"Actually, Mom—" Trace set his cup back down "—I don't. But I think, in a very roundabout way, you're asking me if I approve of you and Stephen dating."

"I wouldn't say we were *dating* exactly," Lilah said, blushing. "Just a couple of dinners, to talk about business, of course. But he has expressed an interest in me, on a more, ah, personal level."

Trace wasn't certain what his mother meant by "personal," but he did know that this conversation was beginning to make him downright uncomfortable. There were some things children simply did not want to discuss with their parents.

"If you want to go out with Stephen, Mom, you should."

Lilah stared at her tea. "It's barely been seven months since your father was killed. You know what people might say."

Trace lifted a brow. "Since when does Lilah Ashton give a damn what people might say?"

"I don't suppose I ever did," Lilah said with a shrug of her shoulder. "I think I'm more worried for Stephen than I am myself. I learned a long time ago how to ignore and deflect gossip, but Stephen, well, he's a good, honorable man. I would hate to cause any problems for him, and let's face it, scandal goes hand in hand with the Ashton name."

How true it was, Trace thought, but for his mother to display more concern for someone other than herself showed tremendous change on her part. "I doubt there's anyone outside our family who knows that better than Stephen. He can handle himself."

"I loved your father with all my heart." Lilah dropped her gaze and sighed. "But I realize now it was a selfish, possessive love. I knew he saw other women, but I had my house and children and everything money could buy. I thought that was all I needed."

"And now?" Trace asked.

"And now I know it isn't."

Trace studied his mother's face, saw the sincerity of her words. "You really like him, don't you?"

The blush rose on her cheeks again. "Not many people get a second chance in life. I'm so afraid I'll mess it up."

"You won't." He covered her hand with his. "And even though you don't need it, you have my official permission to date Stephen."

She dropped her gaze. "Stephen has a meeting tonight in San Francisco. He asked me to go with him."

Trace nodded. "All right."

"I thought...we thought—we'd come back tomorrow morning."

Tomorrow? Good God, this was *definitely* something he didn't want to discuss with his mother. He picked up his glass of water and took a long gulp to clear the dryness in his throat. What the hell was he supposed to say? He knew she was waiting, anxious for his approval.

"Okay, well, have a nice time."

Lilah's shoulders relaxed, then tears filled her

eyes. She reached out and laid her palm on his cheek. "I don't deserve you."

The depth of emotion in his mother's voice and touch surprised and embarrassed him. He couldn't remember a time he'd ever seen her so genuinely open with her feelings and he wasn't quite certain how to respond. "Mom—"

"You don't have to say anything, dear." Lilah smiled, then patted his cheek. "I won't even ask you about the woman I saw driving away from your apartment this morning."

Trace felt the blood leave his face. Dammit! So she *had* seen Becca leave.

"Excuse me, Mrs. Spencer." Irena, the Ashton Estate's head housekeeper, stood in the doorway of the veranda. With her topknot of plain brown hair, stoic features and gray uniform, the woman gave the impression of a mouse, but everyone who lived and worked at the Estate knew that Irena Hunter was a force to be reckoned with.

Trace silently thanked the woman for saving him from an awkward moment with his mother.

"What is it, Irena?" Lilah asked.

"Mr. Cassidy is on the phone. Shall I take a message?"

Pleasure lit Lilah's face. She started to rise, then

glanced at Trace and sat back down. "Ask Mr. Cassidy if I may return his call, please."

"Go ahead, Mom." Trace downed the rest of his coffee and stood. "I've got to get back to work, anyway."

"Are you sure, dear?"

"I'm sure." He kissed his mother's cheek. "Tell Stephen I said hello."

Smiling, Lilah hurried from the room. Trace stared after her for several long moments. Had she known it was Becca leaving his apartment this morning? he wondered.

Did it matter if she did?

Not one little bit.

Five years ago, when Becca had broken their engagement, his mother had cried and been furious that her son's heart had been broken. To his annoyance, she'd fussed over him for months, pushed him at every available, wealthy socialite within a two-hundred-mile radius. He'd made an attempt at dating a couple of the women, but he simply hadn't been interested.

Now, at least temporarily, Becca was back. He'd told himself he'd only wanted her in his bed so he could get her out of his system. But that hadn't happened.

And now, Trace realized, he wasn't so sure what he wanted at all.

It was just dinner, Becca told herself on the sidewalk outside Morelli's. A quick bite to eat, a little conversation. Nothing formal or fancy, just a couple slices of pizza. Tonight, she'd be home and in bed early.

Alone.

All day, she'd barely been able to work. How could she, with thoughts of Trace constantly intruding? Over and over, she'd replayed last night in her mind. Every passionate kiss, every urgent whisper, every soul-shuddering touch. Even now, standing in the chilly night air, her blood warmed with the memory.

Forcing her mind back to the present, she inhaled a deep breath and went inside the busy pizzeria. Nothing had changed since she'd been here last. The same red vinyl and chrome booths. The same wall mural of an Italian vineyard. The same mouth-watering scent of herbs and tomato sauce.

Trace sitting at the same booth where they used to sit.

When he looked up and smiled, her heart stumbled.

Pull yourself together, she scolded. Squaring her shoulders, she made her way toward him, grateful that the other diners were busy with their food or watching Monday night football on the wall-mounted television.

Feeling strangely shy and more than a little nervous, she slid across from him in the booth. When their knees bumped, she quickly tucked her legs into the corner. If he noticed, he didn't comment.

"Hi." Feverishly she worked on something clever to say beyond that when Trace rose, slid onto the seat beside her and dropped his mouth on hers.

Her mind simply went blank.

He kissed her hard and quick, then pulled away and moved back to his side of the booth. Shocked, all she could do was stare.

"I've been thinking about doing that all day." He sipped from the bottle of beer sitting in front of him. "Just thought I'd get it out of the way."

Would she forever be off balance around him? she wondered. A simple kiss and she suddenly couldn't think, couldn't breathe? Was she really that defenseless against him?

Annoyed at the thought, she lifted her chin and met his gaze.

"I'm not sleeping with you tonight, Trace." She felt a smidgen of satisfaction at the surprised lift of his brow. "Just thought I'd get *that* out of the way."

He grinned at her. "Can I at least get a ride home? I just dropped my car off at the body shop to replace a fender."

"I suppose so." She slipped out of her coat. "If you can jump from a speeding car."

He reached across the table, touched the tips of her fingers with his. "Do I make you nervous, Becca?"

A tingle ran through her when he softly moved his fingers over hers. Darn it! Why couldn't she lie to this man? "Yes."

"Good."

There it was again. The slightest touch and she could feel her bones melting. He more than made her nervous, she thought and pulled her hands away. He scared her to death.

"One large pepperoni." A short-haired brunette wearing a diamond stud in her left nostril slid the pizza onto the table.

Becca glanced at Trace. She hadn't been certain she'd show up, but apparently he had been. She hated being so predictable, but after last night, she figured it was a little late to be coy.

"Something to drink?" the waitress asked Becca while she dished up two slices of pizza.

"Iced tea, please."

The pizza smelled as good as it looked, and Becca realized how hungry she was. She pulled off a slice of pepperoni and popped it in her mouth, then took a bite of the warm cheesy dough.

Trace hadn't been the only thing she'd missed, she thought with a moan. No one made a pizza like this in L.A.

Chuckling, Trace dug into his own piece of pie. "Tell me about your business."

She thought for a moment while she chewed, decided the topic was safe enough. "Not much to tell, really. The first year I survived on royalties from stock photographs, then I finally got my foot in the door shooting layouts for a couple of food magazines. Six months ago I landed an account with a vineyard in Santa Barbara and that led me to Glen Ivy, then Whitestone."

"And Louret?"

She glanced up at him, took a sip of the iced tea the waitress had just set on the table. So he had heard about Louret. "I'm not officially hired yet. Your—"

she fumbled "—ah, Mercedes is looking at my proposal."

"You can call her my sister," Trace said evenly. "We've all come to terms with the fact we share our father's blood. We, or I should say, our lawyers, are dealing with the terms of all the rest."

"You mean that they're contesting the will?" she asked, then bit her lip. "I'm sorry. That's none of my busincss."

He smiled. "It's no secret. My father's offspring, like his holdings, are as extensive as they are complicated. It's going to take some time to sort everything out."

Becca considered what she was about to say carefully. As much as she'd prefer to avoid the subject of their past, she decided that Trace should know his name had come up in her meeting with Mercedes. "She—your sister, asked me if it would be a problem for me to work for Louret."

"Why would it be a problem?"

"She knew that we were, that we used to be—" God. She couldn't even say it.

"Engaged?" he finished for her.

Becca nodded. "She was concerned that I might be uncomfortable working for them."

"I see." Trace lifted a brow, then leaned back in his seat. "And what did you say?"

"That whatever my relationship had been with you, it would not affect my work."

He picked up his beer and tossed back a swig. "Are you asking me if I mind?"

"I'm not asking you anything," she said, stiffening, wondered if maybe she *had* wanted to know how he felt about her working for Louret. "I just thought, given the situation, you should know."

He set his beer down carefully. "And just what *is* the situation, Becca?"

Dammit. She'd fallen right into that one. She could pretend she didn't understand what he meant, or she could say there was no situation, which would imply that last night hadn't meant anything to her.

When his cell phone rang and saved her from answering his question, relief poured through her. Frowning, Trace pulled the phone from his jeans' pocket and snapped it open.

"Yeah," he practically barked into the phone, then straightened quickly as he listened. "I'm on my way."

"What's wrong?" she asked when he hung up.

"Megan's water just broke." Trace's hand shook as he tossed several bills onto the table. "We need to get her to the hospital."

The waiting could kill a guy, Trace decided.

He paced outside the examination room the nurses

had wheeled Megan into, wondered how five minutes could seem like five hours. There'd been a constant flow of activity coming and going from the room, but he had no idea what was going on, only that his sister was in labor and for the past thirty minutes, since Simon had dropped Megan off at the nail salon in town, he'd been MIA.

The sound of a muffled moan from inside the room turned Trace's blood to ice.

Thank God, Becca was in there with Megan. Though there'd been a moment of awkwardness when they'd picked his sister up at the salon, it had been quickly forgotten when Megan had nearly doubled over with a contraction. Becca had squeezed Megan's hand and kept talking to her through the pain, then kept talking all the way to the hospital. Trace had white-knuckled the steering wheel and kept his eyes on the road.

He knew nothing about labor and babies. It wasn't something he'd ever needed to think about, and the fact was, everything about it scared the hell out of him. Sure, he'd planned on having a couple of his own one day, after his sisters had popped out a few. By then, he figured he'd be a pro.

He heard another moan, then a curse word. Megan

never cursed. She was always in control, always held it together.

Dammit! Trace dragged a hand through his hair. Where *was* Simon?

Simon hadn't let Megan out of his sight for the past two weeks and now suddenly the man couldn't be found anywhere. Trace had called his mother, then remembered she was in San Francisco with Stephen, and the best he could do was leave a message on her cell phone. He'd also tried Paige, but she hadn't answered her phone, either. It was like everyone in his family had fallen into a hole somewhere.

Trace glanced at his wristwatch again. Six minutes.

Dammit, dammit, *dammit!*

"Trace!"

He spun in time to see Simon and Paige come flying around the corner together.

"Where is she?" Simon demanded.

"Number five."

Simon rushed past Trace and disappeared into the room.

"Where were you?" Trace asked Paige.

"I met Simon at the jewelry store. He wants to surprise Megan with a necklace after the baby is born and he wanted my input. We didn't realize there was no service on our phones until a few minutes ago." Paige grabbed Trace's arm. "Just tell me how she is."

"She's doing fine," Becca said, stepping out of the room.

Paige blinked. "Becca?"

"It's a long story." At the moment, the last thing he wanted to do was go into an explanation of why Becca was here. "We'll talk later."

"I'll hold you to that." Paige looked from Becca to Trace, then back to Becca. "How's she doing?"

"She's doing great." Becca smiled. "You're just in time to welcome your niece into the world."

Paige's eyes widened, then she hurried into the room. Trace felt the blood rush from his head. He took hold of Becca's arms. "Really?"

Becca nodded. "Really."

"But we just got here." Trace shook his head. "Simon just got here. Babies are supposed to take hours, days, according to my mother."

"Apparently, Megan had been having low back pain and didn't realize she was in labor," Becca said. "When her water broke, that sped things up even more."

"But still—" Trace gulped in air "—she can't be, I mean, how could she—"

At the sound of a baby crying, Trace stared in shock at the room, then looked back at Becca. "Is that…did she—" he swallowed hard "—oh, God."

Becca laughed. "Congratulations, Trace. You're an uncle."

Eight

It was nearly ten o'clock when Becca pulled into the main drive of the Ashton Estates. She hadn't had a drop to drink, but she felt wonderfully intoxicated and ridiculously giddy.

The birth of Amber Rose Pearce, seven pounds, six ounces, twenty-one inches long, had caused quite a bit of excitement at the hospital. She may have been two weeks early, but once she decided it was time to be born, she came in like a bright, beautiful rocket. Big rosy cheeks, huge blue eyes, velvety blond hair. And quite an attitude, Becca thought, remembering the baby's tiny clenched fists and irate wail.

It should have been awkward, being part of such an intimate and exciting family event. Becca hadn't seen Megan and Paige in five years, and considering how abruptly she'd broken her engagement to Trace, it would be reasonable to assume that his sisters would feel resentment toward her.

But if they had resented her, or her being there, they certainly hadn't shown it in any way. If anything, both Megan and Paige had seemed pleased that she was there—and more than a little curious, though neither one had actually said anything. But then, they *had* been a little bit busy.

Especially Megan.

"You're smiling."

"What?" She stopped the car in front of Trace's apartment, then glanced over at him. "Oh. I guess I am. It was just so amazing."

"It was, wasn't it?" He grinned back at her. "Once you get past the scary part."

"You should have seen your face when Simon handed you the baby," she said, laughing. "I would have thought he'd put a ticking bomb in your arms."

"A bomb would have been less terrifying," he admitted. "I still can't believe how tiny she is."

"I appreciate Megan letting me hold her, too." Becca had never experienced anything like it in her life. The incredible smell of a newborn baby, the rose-petal-soft skin, the sweet cooing sounds. Cuddling little Amber had melted Becca's heart, made her yearn and long to hold a baby of her own.

And when she'd watched Trace hold his new niece, saw the look of wonder and adoration on his face, Becca knew it was *his* baby she wanted to hold.

Their baby.

"Come on." Trace reached across the seat and turned off the headlights, then plucked the keys from the ignition. "I believe I can find a bottle of bubbly to celebrate."

"Trace, no—"

But he wasn't listening. He was already out of the car and coming around to open her door, dragging her from behind the wheel and ignoring her protests as he pulled her along with him up the stairs to his apartment. In spite of the little voice telling her to run while she could, her heart told her to stay.

The night air was cold, the sky sparkling with stars, the moon a low-hanging crescent. Silence surrounded them, a sense that for a little while, at least, all was right with the world.

By the time they reached the top of the stairs, she

was laughing and more than a little breathless. She gasped when he unexpectedly wrapped his arms around her waist and kissed her hard, then with a loud whoop, spun her around.

"She has to be the most beautiful baby in the world," he said with a big grin. "I'm an uncle."

"Uncle Trace." She'd never seen this side of him before, Becca realized. The man she'd known five years ago had always kept his emotions in check, had always been in control. "I like the sound of it."

"Yeah. Me, too." He set her back on her feet. "Thank you. For being there."

"It was wonderful."

He stared down at her for a long, heart-stopping moment, then the smile on his face slowly faded. He lowered his head and kissed her, softly, gently, and she thought she might cry from the emotion rippling between them. She knew that the change in him had nothing to do with his feelings for her, but that didn't seem to affect her reaction to his kiss. His lips lightly touched hers, brushed back and forth, then settled tenderly over her mouth.

His tongue, hot and moist, swept over her lips. She struggled to breathe, heard the sound of her pulse thundering in her head.

"Come inside with me," he whispered.

Her heart hammered in her chest, blood raced like liquid fire through her veins. Tonight, she decided, she would listen to her heart.

"Yes."

They tumbled through the front door, wrapped in each other's arms. Need pumped through her, desire sang, resistance melted away. She wanted as she'd never wanted before, and the realization was exhilarating. They moved slowly toward the bedroom, neither one of them wanting to break contact. Her fingers shook while she worked the buttons of his shirt, he tugged her sweater over her head, kissing her again and again.

Clothes lined the hallway, and by the time they toppled onto the bed, they were naked.

Bare skin to bare skin, he rolled her underneath him, kissed her long and deep, until she was gasping for breath.

"I…told…you—" she bit her lip when his mouth moved down her neck "—I wasn't going to…sleep with you tonight."

"We aren't sleeping." He nuzzled that little spot just below her ear.

Smiling, she slid her arms over his shoulders. "True."

He filled his hands with her breasts, caressed her

sensitive, swollen flesh until her nipples hardened, then replaced his hands with his mouth. She arched upward on a low moan, certain she could die from the pleasure pulsing through her. His teeth lightly raked her nipple and she moaned softly, dragging her fingers through his thick, dark hair.

She whispered his name, struggled to rein in the emotions spiraling through her. His mouth was warm against her breast, his tongue hot and moist. And so very, very busy.

Did he know how much she needed him? she wondered dimly.

Did she really want him to know?

It frightened her, to give herself to him, not just her body, but her heart. She loved him. She'd never stopped loving him. She knew she never would.

Wrapping her arms tightly around him, she rolled until he was underneath her. She hadn't the courage to say the words, but she would show him.

Even in the dim light of the room, she could see the fierce expression in his eyes when she straddled him. She laid her hands on his broad chest, felt his muscles tense under her touch. Lowering her mouth to his, she kissed him softly, then moved her lips down his neck, savoring the dark, heady taste of his skin.

"Becca..." He took hold of her arms, but she shook her head.

"Let me," she murmured. *Love you,* she finished silently.

His fingers tightened on her skin, then dropped to his sides.

Palms flat, fingers splayed, she moved her hands over his strong shoulders and chest while she caressed him with her lips and teeth. His breathing grew sharp, ragged, his muscles tightened with restrained desire.

Though her own body screamed to feel him inside her, her love and her need to give pleasure kept her focused. She took her time, slowly worked her way down his magnificent body. More than once, he swore, his voice hoarse and rough. When her hands and mouth slid down his hard, flat stomach, he sucked in a breath and jerked underneath her.

He groaned when she moved lower still, then grasped her shoulders. Velvet steel, she thought. Powerful, arousing. Need—urgent, raw, wild—surged out of control.

"Dammit." His fingers dug into her arms. "That's it."

She hadn't time to resist before she found herself on her back. His hands raced up her arms, circled her wrists and raised them over her head.

Her heart pounded furiously, she gasped for breath, then cried out when he entered her in one hard, deep stroke. She met him, wrapped her legs around him and rode the violent wave of passion that consumed them both. He filled her. Her mind, her heart, her body and soul.

Arching upward, she cried out, shuddered again and again. He groaned, his body shaking with the force of his release.

While she waited for the world to find balance again, she held him close and fought back the moisture gathering in her eyes—tears of joy, she realized, then smiled.

Tears of hope.

He watched her sleep.

Light spilled into the bedroom from the hallway and washed across the room in a golden glow. The silence of midnight, smooth and warm and soft, closed around them.

Elbow bent, head propped in his hand, Trace lay on his side and studied her face. The delicate arch of her brow. The straight line of her cute nose. The sexy curve of her lips.

Her hair fanned across the pillow and, unable to resist, he traced one silky curl with his fingertip. He liked the way she wore it now, a little shorter, with a few wispy bangs. But he'd liked it before, too, he remembered, and the image of Becca on a swing jumped into his mind. He could still hear her laugh, see the sunlight in her billowing hair as he'd pushed her higher and higher.

He smiled at the memory. They'd picnicked at the park. She'd packed ham sandwiches and potato salad. He'd brought a blanket and a bottle of Pinot Noir. They'd stayed until dark, kissed under the stars, talked about their dreams. She wanted to take pictures and travel. He wanted to create his own winery and label.

And then she'd left.

His smile faded. When he saw her again, he'd told himself he'd wanted her in his bed to get her out of his system. After he had, he'd been certain he could walk away without a second thought.

Revenge? he wondered. Or had he simply wanted to punish her? Both, he decided.

He watched her roll to her side and sigh, then burrow her cheek into the pillow. Something stirred inside him. Lust, he told himself. Certainly not love. He'd made that mistake once with this woman, let himself be fooled by his emotions. He wouldn't do it again.

This time, he would be the one in control.

Eyes narrowed, muscles tense, he pulled back the bedclothes, watched her eyes flutter open, then moved quickly over her. He held her gaze when he filled her, thrust his hips hard and deep, held her gaze as the rhythm built, faster, harder, until they were both gasping.

His need bordered on violent. He grasped her hips, plundered her body savagely. When her eyes glazed over and she arched upward on a mindless, shuddering moan, he held back, refusing to give in to the fierce need ripping at his gut. Pleasure turned to pain and still he waited, his thrusts hard and fast inside the tight, hot glove of her body.

Her nails raked over his shoulders, her legs tightened around his hips. On a guttural moan, he threw his head back, his body convulsing with the blinding force of his release.

Seconds…minutes passed before he could move, then he rolled to his back and took her with him.

She woke slowly, with the early morning sun on her face and the scent of coffee in the air. The bed beside her was empty, the sheets rumpled and cool. Becca slid her hand over the smooth, beige-striped cotton, felt the warm wave of contentment ripple upward through her fingers and settle into her bones.

Something had happened last night. Well, other than the obvious, she thought, smiling at the memory of making love with Trace. He'd been tender, yet forceful. Patient, but demanding. Heat rushed through her as she remembered her own lack of inhibition. She'd never considered herself a wanton woman, but she certainly had been last night.

Her smile widened.

Wickedly, wonderfully, gloriously wanton.

But there'd been something else happening between them last night besides sex. An undefinable shift in the careful and tentative relationship that she and Trace had established. The possibility that maybe, just maybe....

She hugged her pillow, afraid to even finish the thought. What if she'd read the situation wrong? What if he'd simply been caught up in the excitement of becoming an uncle? What if she'd wanted so desperately to believe he felt something for her beyond the physical, that she'd simply imagined it?

And what if she hadn't?

With a groan, she sat on the edge of the bed and stretched her sore, stiff muscles. Her eyes widened at the sight of a darkening bruise on her thigh, and she blushed at the intensity of their lovemaking, realized that she'd just as likely left marks on Trace, too.

She dressed quickly, decided she would shower at

home before she went to work. She also decided she would pick up a present for Megan's baby and take it over to the hospital later, though the possibility of running into Trace's mother made Becca's stomach tighten.

Lilah Ashton had never openly snubbed her, if anything, she'd been exceedingly polite. But Becca had known the woman hadn't wanted her to marry Trace, and it had hurt, just as much as it had hurt her that her own mother had been opposed to their engagement.

It should have been so simple. She'd loved Trace so much, and she had been so certain he'd loved her. In the beginning, Becca had naively, and foolishly, thought that with time, their parents would come to accept their relationship, then eventually be happy for them.

But that had never happened. And it had only seemed that as the days became weeks, then months, Trace's parents, and even her mother had become more determined than ever to break them up. Five years ago, Becca hadn't been strong enough to stand up to them.

Was she strong enough now?

Sighing, she made her way to the kitchen, found Trace rummaging through the back of his refrigerator. He was shirtless and the jeans he wore, faded, the back pockets nearly worn through. Great butt, she thought, watching him from the doorway. Lean waist, wide, muscled shoulders. What woman wouldn't want this man for a lover? When he straightened and she noticed the scratches on those wide, strong shoulders, her cheeks warmed. So she *had* left marks on him, she realized, and bit her bottom lip.

"Good morning," she said, heard the breathless tone in her voice. A carton of eggs in his hand, he turned and smiled at her. Something fluttered in her stomach.

"You're not supposed to be awake yet," he reprimanded.

"I'm not?"

"Nope." He set the eggs on the counter, then pulled out a cube of butter and what looked like a package of shredded cheddar cheese. "Not until I've made you breakfast."

He was making her breakfast? The Trace Ashton she'd known hadn't even owned a can opener. The flutter she'd felt in her stomach moved up to her heart. "You cook now?"

With a shrug, he plucked an egg out of the carton, then—one-handed—he cracked it open into a bowl sitting on the counter. "I'm not sure you'd exactly call it cooking, but I've learned to master an omelette and toast."

He cracked another egg, then cursed as he fished a piece of shell out of the bowl. She moved to the counter beside him, couldn't resist sliding her hand up his bare arm, then pressing her lips to his shoulder. His skin was warm, the scent musky and arousing. "I'm very impressed."

"Yeah?" He twisted and dropped his mouth to hers, a long, sensual kiss that left them both breathing heavier, then he straightened, opened a kitchen drawer and wiggled an eyebrow. "I even have my own whip."

She laughed when he pulled the utensil out of the drawer and waved it at her.

Helping herself to coffee, she wandered the kitchen while he beat the eggs. It felt so familiar, so comfortable, to be here with him. It felt like…home, she realized.

She stood at the kitchen window, sipped her coffee as she glanced out at the rows of bare grape vines, knew that in spring, the view would be an explosion of varying shades of brilliant green.

"There's been a lot of talk about a new Cabernet and label you're introducing," she mentioned.

"Ah, a spy in my midst." He held out his arms in surrender. "Go ahead. Do what you must to get information out of me."

She rolled her eyes at his foolishness. "I think

you've got the other wineries worried you'll snatch up all the awards this year."

"We intend to," he said with a firm nod. "I could arrange a private tasting for you, if you'd like. How 'bout Friday night through Sunday?"

"A three-day tasting?" She raised a brow. "For one wine?"

"This is a wine like nothing you've ever tasted." His gaze slid over her. "Luscious grapes, smooth tannins, supple texture. And a long, long finish."

Becca shivered at his description, and especially liked the long finish part. So *tempting,* she thought, then glanced away from him. She'd wanted to put this off, but knew she couldn't. "I won't be here, Trace."

He stilled. "Oh?"

"I'm finished with the Whitestone shooting," she said as calmly as she could muster. "I need to get back to L.A."

"I see." His shoulders were stiff when he turned back to the eggs. "What about the Louret job?"

"They haven't hired me yet, and even if they do, I wouldn't start for a couple of months."

He grabbed a pan from under the counter, set it carefully on the stove and fired up the flame. "I figured you'd be here until after Christmas."

"I wish I could, but I have to get two proposals out before the end of the year." She forced a smile. "Gotta pay the bills."

Butter sizzled when he dropped a slice onto the hot pan. She hated the sudden silence between them and the cold that had seemed to creep into the room. But still, she wondered. Did it—did *she*—matter enough to him that he would ask her to stay? And if he did, what would she say?

Yes.

Her fingers tightened on her coffee cup while the silence stretched and the eggs bubbled in the pan. She hadn't even realized she'd been holding her breath until he turned to her.

"You don't have to leave, Becca."

Her pulse raced at his words, her heart leaped. But she said nothing, just kept her eyes steady with his intense green gaze.

He turned back to the eggs. "I was going to talk to you about it, but things got a little crazy the past few days."

Crazy, she thought. Yes. They *had* gotten crazy. "Talk to me about what?" she asked hesitantly. Hopefully.

"I've been considering a new design company to run the promotion for Ashton Estates," he said evenly. "I thought you might be interested in handling all of our advertising and marketing."

She furrowed her brow, certain she hadn't heard him right. "What?"

"You're good at what you do, Becca. Very good. I'd like to hire your company to work exclusively for Ashton Estate Winery." He kept his gaze on the omelette, sprinkled cheese on the eggs and flipped one side over. "You could set up a studio here in Napa."

"You mean, move here?" she asked carefully.

"Yes." He slid the eggs onto a plate.

"To work for you."

"For the winery."

"Exclusively."

"Yes."

She stared at him, felt the bubble of joy in her chest burst. This couldn't be happening. *Not again,* she thought.

Not with Trace.

"I'll have to think about it," she said stiffly as the pain sliced sharply through her. When he turned toward her, offering her the plate of food, she was terrified she might be sick.

"You eat it," she managed to say through the dryness in her throat. "I have to leave."

He frowned at her. "What's wrong?"

"I'm running late, Trace. Really, I've got to go."

"Becca—"

"I'll call you later." She turned, knew she had to get away quickly. She grabbed her keys from the front entry table where Trace had dropped them last night and hurried down the stairs.

"Becca, wait a minute, dammit," he called from the doorway.

She didn't answer him, just got in her car and drove away through the haze of tears.

What the hell had he done? Trace thought, staring after Becca as she pulled away. Dammit, anyway! He'd offered her a job—so what? She'd had no problem five years ago when his father had handed her a check, why should him offering a job bother her so much now?

But the look on her face, the shock and disgust, had slammed into his gut like an angry truck driver's fist.

He'd hurt her, he realized.

Confused, he scrubbed a hand over his face. So maybe he hadn't thought this completely through. Actually he hadn't *thought* about it at all. He'd simply panicked when she'd said she was leaving. Offering her a job here in Napa had seemed the most logical thing to do. She could "pay her bills" and she wouldn't be so damn far away.

But there'd been something else in her eyes. Something that had bothered him more than anything else.

Disappointment?

Dammit, *dammit!*

He stomped back into his apartment and slammed the door. *She'd* been the one who'd disappointed him five years ago. *She'd* been the one who'd taken money from his father, then walked out and never looked back. He still had the canceled check, signed by her.

He needed it now, needed to hold it in his hand, look at it. Needed the reminder that money and her career had been more important to her than him. He stormed into his home office and pulled the check out of the lower right-hand drawer, stared at it for what felt like the millionth time.

Becca Marshall. One hundred thousand dollars. Her signature, with its distinct and curly *B*, ending with a swirl after the final *L*.

Something was wrong, he thought, but he didn't know what it was. After what had just happened, he couldn't very well go to Becca and confront her.

There was only one person he could confront. It might be five years too late, he realized, but today, he would finally have the truth.

He picked up the phone and dialed.

Nine

Becca parked her car on the hilltop that overlooked Napa Valley. From her vantage point, the Valley became a sea of vineyards, with roads burrowing not only through the flatland, but on the mountainside, as well. Tall oaks dotted the landscape and rugged hills rose high above the valley floor.

She'd found this spot on a photography field trip in her senior year of high school. On a clear day like this morning, it was a photographer's dream. She'd brought Trace here once, wanting to share her little slice of heaven with him. He'd teased her that she had stars in her eyes.

Maybe she had.

She'd known who Trace's family was before she'd met him, had heard the scandalous talk about his father. According to the rumors, Spencer Ashton had been a ruthless, heartless son of a bitch who would sell his grandmother for a buck.

She'd never really believed the gossip, at least, not completely. How could any man who'd raised a son as loving and caring as Trace be that calloused? There had to be *some* good in Spencer, Becca had thought. Some kernel of kindness.

How wrong she'd been.

She would never forget the day Spencer had handed her that check. She'd been so confused, had stared at the huge amount of money, not understanding what was happening. Even after Spencer had explained, she'd still been dazed.

The anger had come much later.

He'd shattered her life that horrible day, taken something precious away from her she'd never been able to get back.

Trust.

But despite everything, she'd never believed that Trace was like his father. How could she have fallen in love with him if he was?

She'd let herself get close to him again, let herself fall in love all over again.

And this morning, like his father, Trace had tried to buy her.

A dull, heavy pain squeezed her chest, made it difficult to breathe.

He hadn't even been subtle about it, she thought miserably. He'd thought he could "hire her," have her move to Napa and she'd be available whenever he snapped his fingers for a quick roll in the hay. Her hands tightened around the steering wheel. This Trace, she thought, was a man she didn't know at all. A man she didn't want to know.

And still, idiot that she was, she loved him.

She didn't try to fight the tears. What use was it? They would come sooner or later and she'd just as soon get it out of the way.

Because this time, she thought, setting her teeth, she wouldn't run. This time she would face him. This time, she'd look him in the eye, rant and yell if she felt like it, and she'd tell him exactly what she thought.

Trace knocked on Elaine Marshall's front door, then rang the doorbell twice. It was barely nine o'clock and he knew Becca's mother would be sleeping. He didn't care.

When the door finally opened, Elaine stood on the other side. She tugged on the belt of her blue robe, then ran her fingers through her rumpled hair and frowned at him.

"Becca's not here." Her voice was rough with sleep.

"I'm not here to see Becca, Mrs. Marshall." Tension crackled off his words. "I'm here to see you."

"What's wrong?" Elaine quickly looked past Trace, then narrowed her eyes with concern. "Is Becca all right?"

"Physically, I'm sure she's fine." He prayed she was, anyway. He couldn't get the image of her eyes, like an injured animal's, out of his mind. "I need to talk with you."

Shaking her head, Elaine started to close the door. "I'm sorry, Trace, but this isn't a good time."

Trace put his hand on the knob to hold the door, then reached into the pocket of his jacket and pulled out the check. "I doubt there is a good time, Mrs. Marshall." He held the check close to Elaine's face. "We'll talk now."

Her eyes widened a fraction, then her lips pressed into a thin line. Nodding slowly, she stepped aside and opened the door.

"Why don't we go in the kitchen?" she suggested.

"I just talked to my mother," he said following her. "I know the truth."

Elaine dragged in a long, slow breath, then moved to an end cupboard and pulled out a bottle of bourbon and a glass. "Can I offer you something?"

"No."

She poured two fingers, then took a swallow and turned back to face him. "It was five years ago, Trace. Why don't we just leave it alone?"

"Leave it alone?" Rage swelled in his chest. He was still trying to absorb what his mother had told him, and now Becca's mother had the nerve to tell him to *leave it alone*? "Like hell we will."

"You don't understand, Trace." Elaine closed her eyes. "Until you're a parent, you can't understand the need to protect."

"You call what my father and mother did, what you did, *protection*?" He struggled to rein in his anger. "Bribery, lies, manipulating. How the hell is that protecting someone you say you love?"

"Don't you dare question my love for my daughter." Elaine slammed her glass down on the counter. "You were both too young, from two different worlds, living in fantasyland. Once the lust faded, you would have grown tired of her. I'm not sorry for what I did. I'd do it all over again in a heartbeat if it would keep my baby safe."

"What would you do, Mom?"

Trace turned at the sound of Becca's voice behind him. *Thank God she was all right.* As desperately as he wanted to snatch her into his arms, he knew that right now she would only push away from him. There was nothing he could do to stop this, wouldn't even if he could. As hard as it was, for the first time in five years, both he and Becca would know the truth.

Trace looked at Elaine, watched her eyes widen as Becca moved into the room. Grabbing the lapel of her robe, she forced a smile. "Becca, there you are, honey. Trace and I were worried about you."

Becca kept her eyes on her mother. "What did you do?"

"We should talk about this later." Panic edged Elaine's voice. "Wait for things to calm down."

"We've waited long enough." Trace laid the check on the stovetop. "Tell her."

Becca glanced at the check, and her face turned ashen. "Where did you get that?"

"My father gave it to me five years ago."

"He gave it to you?"

He nodded. "The day you left."

"So you knew what he'd done," she whispered. "You *knew*?"

All those days, weeks, she'd waited for him, she remembered. Even in Italy, she'd imagine she saw him in a crowd, or sitting in a restaurant. Every time the phone rang, her pulse raced, every knock on her door, her stomach would twist. She'd hoped, prayed, it would be him. But it never was.

She looked at him, waited for him to answer her, realized that he was staring at her mother.

"Tell her," Trace said tightly.

"Tell me what?" Becca watched her mother reach for the glass on the counter and take a drink. Why was her hand shaking so badly? "Mom, what did you do?"

When Elaine swiveled her face away, Trace turned the check over. Becca moved closer, saw the signature. *Her* signature, she realized.

"I—I never signed this." She frowned darkly and looked at Trace. "I don't understand."

"You threw this back in my father's face," he said quietly, "and you told your mother what he'd done."

"I was crying when she came home. She knew something was wrong." Becca closed her eyes and rubbed at her temples. "I had to tell someone, but I couldn't tell you. I didn't want to hurt you or cause more problems."

"Trace, for God's sake, can't you see you're upsetting her?" Elaine moved toward Becca. "Sweetheart, I can see you're exhausted. Rest for a while and then we'll—"

"No!" Becca held out a hand and stepped back from her mother. *"Tell me what you did."*

Elaine's face twisted with fear. She clutched a hand to her throat and slowly met her daughter's gaze. Her voice was barely audible, but in the tense silence, her words thundered. "I went to Spencer."

"You went to Trace's father?" Becca narrowed her eyes in confusion.

Elaine nodded. "I took the check and deposited it in an account I'd set up for you when you were little."

The admission was like a slap in her face. Gasping, Becca lifted a hand to her cheek. "And you—you signed my name?"

Elaine nodded stiffly. "Yes."

Becca's mind raced back to that awful day. Spencer offering her money. Her mother coming in and hugging her, telling her that Trace didn't deserve her, that his family would never let them be happy. "So when you told me I should go to Europe and forget Trace, that you had money put away my grandmother had left me..."

"I'm sorry, baby," Elaine said raggedly. "I lied to you."

Oh, God. Becca squeezed her eyes shut. "How could you?"

"Because I agreed with him." Elaine lifted her chin. "You and Trace are from two different worlds. You might have been happy for a few months, but then I knew you'd be miserable."

"You *knew* I'd be miserable?" Becca stared at her mother in disbelief. "That's what you honestly believed?"

"Everyone knew what kind of man Spencer was." Disdain dripped from Elaine's voice. "Why would his son be any different? He didn't deserve you."

"Trace loved me," Becca whispered. "I loved him."

"Love." Elaine spat the word. "Baby, believe me, it doesn't exist. You were infatuated. He was in lust. It would only be a matter of time before he broke your heart and crushed your spirit."

"Is that what my father did to you?" Becca asked quietly. "Crushed your spirit?"

"Your father has *nothing* to do with this."

Elaine reached for the bottle of bourbon and started to pour herself another drink. Becca moved across the kitchen, gently took the bottle and glass away and set them on the counter.

"Yeah, Mom." She looked at her mother. "I think he has everything to do with this."

Elaine met her daughter's steady gaze, then her face slowly crumpled and she dropped her head into her hands with a sob. "I gave him everything. My heart, my soul, my body. When he found out I was pregnant, he ran off with my cousin."

Part of Becca wanted to hold her mother, to comfort, but the other part of her, the part that was too raw, the part that was angry and hurt, wouldn't let her.

"Sweetheart—" Elaine reached out and cupped Becca's face in her hands "—I took that money for you. So you could make a life for yourself away from here. I just wanted what was best for you. That's all I've ever wanted."

Shaking her head, Becca removed her mother's hands from her face. "You had no right."

"I know." Tears streamed down Elaine's cheeks. "I know. I'm so sorry."

"I'm going outside to talk to Trace." Becca had to swallow the thickness in her throat before she could speak again. "I'd appreciate it if you'd give us some time."

Elaine nodded, then glanced at Trace. "I—I'm sorry."

His face was a cold, hard mask. He said nothing,

just turned and followed Becca onto the front porch, then sat down beside her on the front step.

Without touching, they sat shoulder to shoulder, neither one of them speaking. The morning air was cool; a breeze shivered through the tops of the elm trees across the street. Two young boys rode their skateboards down the sidewalk while a black labrador trotted behind.

Her entire life had been shattered, and still, life went on.

She stared at the house across the street, wondered why she'd never noticed their front door was painted blue. "You thought I took the money."

"I saw your signature," he said stiffly.

"And you thought I took the money."

"Yes."

She wouldn't have thought it possible to hurt any more than she had this morning. Now, after her mother's confession, and knowing that Trace had believed she'd been bought off, she knew it was possible. The pain, black, intense, razor-sharp, sliced through her.

"I wondered why you never came after me." It felt as if she'd left her body, as if she were standing several feet away, looking at two people she didn't even recognize.

He picked up a stone from the dirt and rolled it in the palm of his hand. "I wondered why you left a note, why you couldn't face me and say goodbye."

"I was afraid."

"Of me?"

"Of everything." Lord, she was exhausted. Every word felt like an effort. "Your father, your money. That we were too different. That one day you would leave me. If I had seen you after your father tried to give me that check, you would have known something had happened. I couldn't tell you what he'd done, it would have only caused more problems, more grief. Where would we have gone from there?" She took in a deep breath and turned her head to look at him. "So I left."

"And you stayed away."

"Two months later I saw your picture in a wine and food magazine, taken at a charity event for cancer. You were with a gorgeous blonde and the article hinted you were engaged. I figured if you were already with someone else, that maybe our parents were right about us."

He shook his head and sighed. "My mother orchestrated the date and the article. I wasn't happy about either one."

"It took me five years to find the courage to come

back here," she said. "I'd convinced myself that I'd moved on, that my feelings for you were in the past. And then I saw you and I knew they weren't."

"Becca, this morning..."

"It doesn't matter." She stood, looked down at him. "I was fooling myself into thinking we might have another chance. Five years ago, now, it's the same. We just can't seem to get it right."

"Come with me." His mouth pressed into a hard line, he rose from the step. "We'll go back to my place and figure this out."

When he reached for her, she shook her head and stepped back. "It might take me a while, but I intend to pay back every penny my mother took."

"Dammit, Becca." Anger iced over his eyes and tightened his jaw. "This isn't about money."

"No, it's not." She moved backward toward the door, prayed her knees wouldn't give out before she got inside. From somewhere deep inside herself, she found the courage she'd never had.

"Goodbye, Trace."

Inside, she closed the door with a quiet click, then pressed her forehead to the cool wood. When she heard his car start, then drive away, she sank to the floor and cried.

Ten

A shovel in his hands, mud up to his knees, Trace stood in the rain and tunneled through the soaking wet mound of dirt. For every scoop of earth he dug and tossed aside, it seemed as if two took its place. When his shovel thunked against a football-size rock, the reverberation sang smartly up his arms.

Dammit to hell!

He hooked the shovel under the rock and loosened it, then bent and heaved it aside with the growing pile beside the road.

The persistent rain had started two days ago, hard

enough to block up a culvert running under one of the roads that wound through the vineyards. The ensuing flood had nearly washed out the road and created one hell of a mess.

He might have brought one of the field hands to help, but he'd wanted to be alone with his dark mood, and he figured the physical labor would help work off some of his tension.

So far, he'd only become more frustrated.

Becca had gone back to Los Angeles five days ago. Every day, he'd picked up the phone to call her. Every day, he'd hung it up before it rang.

And if he had let it ring, if she had picked up, what the hell would he have said? *I'm sorry I tried to buy you like my father had?*

He'd let her down, her mother had let her down. It seemed that he'd only brought her more hurt by being in her life than being out of it.

How could he have ever believed she'd taken money from his father? His family's money and name had never been important to Becca. If anything, it had made her uncomfortable.

Why hadn't he trusted her?

Rain battered the slicker he wore, pounded on the ground, pooled around his feet. He tossed another shovel of mud aside, cursed the damn rain, cursed the damn mud and cursed himself. Elaine Marshall had been right about one thing, Trace knew. He didn't deserve Becca. He never had.

She was better off without him.

The single story guest house sat comfortably on the east corner of Louret Vineyard. With its peaked slate roof and wooden sides, the structure had a storybook feel to it: lazy vines of English ivy, granite-edged flower beds, a smoke-billowing stone fireplace chimney. A small lake and stand of olive trees in the distance completed the postcard-perfect picture.

Parking his truck in the driveway, Trace shut off the engine, resisted the urge to start the motor up again. *You called her. She knows you're coming and you're here,* he told himself. *Now get your ass out of the car.*

He grabbed the brightly wrapped box on the seat beside him and climbed out of the truck, then pulled up his collar against the light mist of rain. The worst of the storm had finally passed, but the lingering clouds seemed determined to keep the sun at bay.

The scent of woodsmoke mixed with the fragrant aroma of the pine and cedar holiday wreath hanging on the front door, a clear reminder that Christmas was only two days away.

Not that he was in much of a holiday mood. He didn't feel like celebrating, and as far as he was concerned, he'd just be glad when Christmas was done and gone and he could move into the New Year.

From the other side of the door, Trace heard the sound of a child's laugh, then a puppy's shrill bark. He listened for a moment, frowned when he heard the distinct cry of a woman in distress. He knocked, waited anxiously, then knocked again.

He was reaching to open the door when it flew open.

Anna stood on the other side, looking more than a little frazzled. From the top of her short auburn hair, down to her green silk blouse and black cotton slacks, she was covered in what appeared to be flour.

"I am so sorry," Anna sputtered. "We just had a mishap in the kitchen."

At the sound of a happy shriek and frenetic barking, Anna spun around and ran off.

Not sure what to do, Trace glanced around, then stepped inside the house and closed the door behind him.

The cottage had a warm, homey feel to it, Trace thought. The furniture in the living room was rough-hewn and appeared to be hand-crafted, the sofa covered with fat pillows and handmade quilts. A

Christmas tree decorated with shiny glass ornaments and silver garland brightened one corner, and on the dining room table, a trio of colorful nutcrackers stood guard beside a bright red poinsettia.

Trace set the present he'd brought on the living room floor, then followed the sound of the commotion into a small kitchen. In the middle of the floor, a once black puppy ran circles around a giggling, flour-dusted little boy.

"Cabo, no, stop!" Anna tried desperately to grab the excited puppy, but the animal was too quick for her. Trace stepped in and grabbed the overgrown puppy by its collar, then held on tight when the dog squirmed and wiggled.

"Bless you," Anna said, then groaned when she looked at the child sitting on the floor. "Jack, look at you!"

"Mamma!" Jack grabbed handfuls of flour and tossed it in the air. "We made snow!"

Flour covered the boy's red curls, chubby cheeks and jean overalls. Anna lifted Jack up from the floor and set him on his feet, then looked at Trace apologetically.

"I was pouring a bag of flour into a container and I dropped it." Anna pointed a stern finger at the dog. "Cabo, sit!"

Quivering, his big tongue rolling out the side of his large jaws, the puppy reluctantly sat.

"I'm sorry Grant couldn't be here," Anna said brushing flour off Jack's hair and overalls. "A pipe broke at the house we just bought and he's there with the plumber. It's one of those days."

Fine by me, Trace thought. His relationship, or rather, lack of relationship, with his eldest sibling had been strained from the moment the man had shown up in Napa. Meeting with Jack and Anna was enough for one day.

Anna turned Jack to face Trace. "Jack, this is your brother, Trace. Say hello."

The little boy stuck one short, pudgy, flour-covered finger in his mouth and smiled. "Hi, Trace."

"Hi, Jack."

"That's my doggie, Cabo." Jack pointed at the puppy. "Eli gave him to me."

"A man I may never speak to again," Anna grumbled, taking hold of the dog's collar. "I'll just take him out back and brush him off. Jack, why don't you show Trace your train set?"

The child's face lit up, then he grabbed Trace's hand and pulled him to the Christmas tree in the living room. A six car, miniature train with a shiny black engine had been set up to circle the base of the tree.

Jack plopped down on the floor, then patted the space beside him. "You sit here."

Trace did as instructed, felt like a giant sitting next to the little boy. He watched the child start the train rolling, was impressed with the boy's ability to work the controls.

"I'm the conductor," Jack said, pushing levers and buttons. The train whistled and sped along the tracks, 'round and 'round. "You can be the caboose man."

That pretty much summed up his life, Trace thought. The last car on a train that went nowhere.

Trace watched the excitement sparkle in the boy's green eyes. He'd always imagined he'd have a son one day. That he'd buy him his first train set, then sit beside him next to the Christmas tree and argue over who got to run the controls and make the engine puff black smoke.

In that world, his son had his mother's golden-brown eyes and his daughter had her pretty mouth and cute nose. They'd all drink cocoa and read *'Twas The Night Before Christmas* on Christmas eve, leave cookies out for Santa and carrots for the reindeer.

In that world, he would kiss his wife under the mistletoe, then make sweet love to her after the children were fast asleep.

The tiny hand on his arm shook him out of his

thoughts. He blinked, then glanced down at the child looking up at him.

"You want to be the conductor now?" The boy held out the controls. "My mommy says I should share and take turns."

"You'll have to show me how," Trace said.

Jack's little chest puffed out with pride. "You just push this button here like this and move this back and forth."

When Trace made the train move, Jack clapped his hands. "See, you can do it."

The smile on the boy's face and the joy in his eyes made something shift in Trace's chest.

Trace steered the train around the track while Jack bounced up and down, chatting rapidly about Santa Claus and the fireplace and toys and a flurry of other things that Trace couldn't quite understand. But the words didn't seem to matter. Jack's enthusiasm was infectious, and Trace couldn't help but absorb some of the child's excitement over St. Nick's impending visit.

When a knock at the front door started the puppy barking outside, Anna called from the back of the house, "Trace, would you answer that, please? I'll be out in a minute."

There certainly was a flurry of activity in the

household, Trace thought, and realized that had been part of his imaginary world, as well.

"I'll be right back. You take over for me, okay?" Trace handed the controls back to Jack and ruffled his hair, then rose and answered the front door.

Eli.

They stared at each other, both of them surprised. The smile on Eli's face vanished.

"I stopped by to see Jack," Eli said stiffly. "I'll come back later."

"Eli!"

Arms wide, little Jack tore across the room. Eli's smile was back as he swooped the child up and hugged him. "Whatcha doing, buddy?"

"Playing trains with my brother Trace." Jack looked at Eli. "You're my brother, too."

"Yep." Eli set the boy down. "I sure am."

Jack looked up at Trace curiously. "Are you Eli's brother, too, Trace?"

Trace didn't reply. It was one thing to know it, another to actually say it.

Impatient, Jack persisted. "*Are* you Eli's brother, Trace?" he asked again.

Trace met Eli's gaze. "Yes."

The little boy's face broke into a wide smile and he grabbed Eli's hand. "Come play trains with us, Eli."

"I can't right now," Eli said. "Maybe later."

"You *have* to," Jack whined, and tugged on Eli's hand. "Trace and I took turns being conductor and now it's your turn and you—" Eyes wide, the boy stopped suddenly and grabbed himself. "I have to go potty."

With that announcement, Jack turned and ran, calling to his mother. Trace watched the boy disappear down a hallway, then turned and looked at Eli. There was a brief, awkward moment.

"Well, I guess I should go." Eli shifted from one foot to the other. "Tell Jack I'll come by later."

"Why don't you stay?" Trace offered. "Since it's your turn to be conductor and all."

Eli hesitated, then stepped inside the house. "I, ah, heard Megan had her baby last week. They doing okay?"

Trace nodded. "Great. I heard you and Lara got married. Congratulations."

"Thanks."

"Jack says you got him a puppy."

"Anna's not too happy with me about it," Eli admitted.

"Wait till she sees what I got him," Trace said, glancing at the large wrapped box on the floor.

"What's that?"

"A set of drums."

Eli's eyes widened, then he started to laugh. "You're dead meat."

It was almost surreal, Trace realized, having a civil conversation with Eli. Though they'd shared a father, he'd simply never really thought of the man standing here as his brother.

Maybe it was time to change that.

Maybe, just maybe, he thought, it was time to change a lot of things.

The setting was one of romance. Flickering votives, two delicate flutes of bubbling champagne, black caviar on toast points. One rose, deep red, long-stemmed, stretched across the white linen tablecloth, evoking images of love and passion, lust and desire.

Too bad it was only a display.

Becca snapped several more shots of the arrangement she'd designed for the caviar company, then placed her hands in the small of her back and straightened. Stiff from the long workday, she rolled her head one way, then the other, but the tension in her neck and shoulders stubbornly remained.

For the past week she'd spent more time in her tiny studio than she had at home, hoping that work would keep her mind off Trace. It hadn't, of course, but at least it had given her something to do other than curling up in a corner and crying her eyes out.

She flipped off her soft box lights, then straddled a folding chair, rested her chin on her arms and listened to the persistent tick of her wristwatch. She knew it was past seven o'clock, but it didn't matter. She had nowhere to go, no one to be with.

Even if it was Christmas Eve.

She stared at the flickering candles and champagne, thought about the bottle she and Trace had shared the night Megan's baby had been born. It was a night she would never forget. Every kiss, every touch, every whisper, would be etched in her mind forever. As would her forged signature on that check and the fact that Trace had actually thought she'd taken money from his father.

The two people she'd loved most in the world had betrayed her.

The pain would ease one day. With time and distance and a determination to move on with her life. She had all those things in her favor. Trace might have broken her heart, but he hadn't broken her spirit.

Though she was still upset with her mother, Becca ached for her, too. Her anger and bitterness had festered for so many years, blinded her to the possibility of finding love again.

Will that happen to me? Becca thought, then shook her head fiercely. She couldn't let that happen. She *would* get over Trace somehow.

But not right now. Right now, every little piece of her heart felt shattered. Right now, every little piece of her heart still belonged to Trace.

The knock at the door startled her. She wasn't expecting anyone, and she knew that most of the other tenants in the building had left earlier in the day. Frowning, she went to the door and looked through the peephole. She dragged in a slow breath when she saw who it was, then opened the door.

"You aren't answering your phone," her mother said.

"You drove all the way here to tell me that?" In spite of what had happened, she was glad to see her mother, knew it was the first step in healing their wounded relationship.

"Don't be sassy," Elaine reprimanded. "Of course I didn't come here to tell you that. I came here to tell you I love you."

"I love you, too, Mom."

Moisture filled Elaine's eyes, then she straightened her shoulders. "And I didn't drive. I flew."

"You flew?" Becca knew it wasn't easy to fly from Napa to L.A. on a regular day, let alone Christmas Eve. "How did you get a flight?"

"I didn't." Her mother stepped back and glanced over her shoulder. "Lilah did."

Lilah? Becca narrowed her eyes, then opened them wide when Trace's mother moved into doorway. Becca's heart skipped a beat and her jaw went slack.

"Hello, Becca."

"I—I don't understand." Becca finally managed to find her voice.

The two women smiled at each other, but it was Lilah who spoke first. "What Spencer and I did to you five years ago was unforgivable," Lilah said quietly. "But I'm here to ask you for your forgiveness."

"So am I." Elaine bit her bottom lip. "Please, baby, can you forgive us?"

This was unbelievable. Her mother had come here with *Lilah Ashton,* to ask for forgiveness? Becca looked from her mother to Lilah, saw the sincerity of their request.

She'd lost five precious years with Trace. A lifetime. Could she forgive, honestly and completely?

Could she?

No one moved, no one breathed.

Then Becca opened her arms and nodded.

There were more tears and muffled sobs. Tissues came out and were passed around, then more hugs.

Her heart might be broken, Becca thought, but at least it felt lighter.

They were all wiping their eyes when they pulled apart. Becca realized they were still standing in the doorway. "Come in," she said, stepping aside. "I have some champagne, or I could make some coffee."

"We can't, sweetheart." Elaine smiled at Lilah. "Stephen and Lilah are taking me to dinner. He has a friend here in L.A., a widower, and we're meeting him at Spago's."

"You're…going out?" It was first time Becca noticed her mother was wearing a sequinned black jacket over a black dress. Lilah wore a cream-colored cashmere sweater and silk pants. They were actually going out? Together? This entire evening kept getting weirder and more unbelievable by the minute.

What about me? she wanted to say. It was Christmas Eve, for crying out loud!

"We'll see you tomorrow." Elaine kissed Becca's cheek. "Give us a call in the morning at the Bonadventure."

The Bonadventure?

She didn't even ask.

It was too much to absorb, Becca thought, closing the door when they left. She stood there, shaking her head, trying to stop the whirlwind in her brain.

Neither her mother nor Lilah had even mentioned Trace. Did he know they'd come here?

The light rap on the door pulled her out of her thoughts. Maybe they'd been teasing her about going out and leaving her alone, she thought. Still in a daze, Becca opened the door.

And her heart stopped.

Trace stood there, hands in the pockets of his leather jacket. Well, *that* certainly answered the question of whether he knew their mothers had been here. She stared at him, torn between throwing herself in his arms and ranting at him.

She decided to do neither.

"Can I come in?" he asked.

"And if I said no?"

"Then I'd wait out here for you."

The idea of him waiting out in the hall for the next several hours appealed to her, but she stepped aside anyway and closed the door when he moved into the room.

He glanced at the display on the table. "You working?"

"No, I'm having a snack." She really hadn't meant to be sarcastic, it just sort of slipped out. Folding her arms, she released the breath she'd been holding. "I *was* working. Until our mothers showed up."

It encouraged Trace that at least Becca wasn't yelling at him, though he wouldn't blame her if she did. "How did that go?"

"They asked me to forgive them." Her face and her voice softened.

"And?"

"I did."

"I'm glad." He moved closer to her, saw a flicker of apprehension in her eyes. "What about me?"

She turned to her display table, fussed with a toast point. "What about you?"

He leaned in close, breathed in the familiar scent of her and held it in his lungs. "Will you forgive me?"

She stilled, but didn't reply.

"I know I'm an idiot," he said, and meant it. "I was an idiot five years ago and I'm an idiot now. But I swear, I'm working on that."

He thought she smiled at that, but he couldn't see her face.

God, he wanted to see her face.

"Becca." He put his hands on her shoulders and turned her. "I'm sorry for what my father did, but I'm even more sorry that I didn't trust you enough to see the truth, that I didn't come after you and drag you back. I wanted to, I thought about it every day, but my damn pride wouldn't let me."

"I should have told you the truth," she said quietly.

He shook his head. "Could we have really been happy knowing our families were adamantly opposed to our being together? And we both know what kind of man my father was."

She closed her eyes. "But what my mother did. Taking that money, lying to me."

"She did the wrong thing for the right reasons," Trace said tenderly. "She loves you. And if there was one thing she was right about, it was that I didn't deserve you. I still don't, but if you'll give me a chance, I'll spend every day of the rest of our lives making it up to you. I love you, sweetheart. I've always loved you."

There were tears in her eyes when she opened them. "I love you, too."

Lightly, he pressed his lips to hers. "When you said you were going back to Napa, I panicked. I'd lost you once, I couldn't handle the thought of losing you again. Marry me, Becca."

He pulled the ring out of his pocket, watched her eyes widen in surprise.

"My ring," she gasped, and looked up at him. "You kept my ring?"

He slipped it on her finger, where it belonged. "I

couldn't let it go. It was part of you, part of us. Say yes. Please say yes."

Tears streamed down her cheeks as she lifted her hand and stared in wonder at the ring she'd worn five years ago. With a small sob, she leaped upward and wrapped her arms around him. "Yes, *yes!*"

He tasted her tears when she kissed him, pulled her closer and tighter, held her like he'd never held her before. He'd never let go again.

"We'll live anywhere you say," he said, lifting his head. "We can live in this room if you want, though we might want something bigger when the babies come."

"Babies," she whispered, then smiled. "We can probably do better than this, you being a rich guy and all."

"The richest," he murmured, and kissed her again.

She took his face in her hands, happiness glowed in her eyes. "Merry Christmas, Trace."

"Merry Christmas, Becca." He smiled back. "Forever."

Epilogue

The official announcement in the *Napa Valley Register* sent a shock wave through the community that rippled up and down the coast. Some people thought it was a mistake in the printing, some thought it was a bad joke—definitely one of poor taste.

It simply wasn't possible that Ashton Estate Winery and Louret Vineyards were merging.

Even Trace, who'd placed the announcement himself, found the news astonishing.

He stood at the entrance of the family room, scanned the faces of everyone who'd been able to join in the celebration. By the fireplace, Megan stood with a sleeping Amber in her arms and talked babies with Mercedes while Simon discussed business with Cole and Jared. Sitting on the sofa, Anna and Grant shared tales of little Jack's latest exploits with Paige and Matt while Jillian and her husband, Seth, looked at photographs of the boy's Christmas day excitement.

Eli, standing by the French doors that led to the breakfast room, had his arm draped possessively around his wife, Lara's shoulders, who was deep in a conversation with Cole's wife, Daisy.

If this group had been gathered under the same roof one year ago, Trace thought, there was no doubt blood would have been shed.

They'd all been tentative of his offer at first, Trace knew, even a bit suspicious. They still had a long way to go before they really knew each other. But they were already family, and he had the feeling that before long, they would be friends, as well.

The past week had involved a dozen meetings, a mountain of paperwork and what felt like hundreds of signatures, but the lawyers had ironed out all the details and it was a done deal: Ashton Estate Winery and Louret Vineyards would now be Kindred Estate Vineyards.

The legacy of greed and avarice that Spencer Ashton had left would now be buried with him. There'd be a fresh start, Trace thought. The estate and its vast holdings would be divided equally, and his mother, who'd left yesterday for a week in Hawaii with Stephen, would keep her beloved house.

United, they stood stronger, in family and in business. The Ashton name and Kindred Vineyards would be a force to be reckoned with.

But this time, a positive force, Trace resolved.

"Hey, you." Becca came up behind him and slipped her arms around his waist. "It's almost midnight."

Smiling, he pulled her close. She'd come back to Napa with him on Christmas day and stayed, made the decision to move her studio to Napa. They'd set their wedding date for June, but not a day, not an hour, went by he didn't wish it was already here.

He leaned down and whispered in her ear, "How 'bout we go somewhere private to start the new year? It's too crowded here."

"Better get used to it." Becca smiled. "It's your family."

His family. Trace glanced around the room again, still trying to absorb the enormity of it all, then looked down at Becca. That she was here, by his side, where she belonged, was the most amazing thing of all.

"Come on." He took her arm and pulled her out onto the veranda.

"Trace, we can't—"

Outside, he dropped his mouth over hers to smother her protest and kissed her deeply, until she finally sighed and melted against him.

"I have something for you," he murmured, then pulled a slender, black velvet box from his jacket pocket.

"Trace, you shouldn't—oh, my God." Her eyes widened when he opened the lid. *"Trace."*

Diamonds surrounded the ruby pendant, sparkled under the soft lights.

"I was going to wait until later." He lifted the necklace from the box. "But I want you to wear it now. Turn around."

"It's beautiful," she whispered breathlessly when he secured the clasp, then turned back to face him. "But you shouldn't have."

That's something *you* better get used to," he said, grinning. "I want to give you everything."

Tears filled her eyes as she touched his cheek. "Don't you know you already have?"

He bent to kiss her again, but his lips had barely touched hers when he heard a man clearing his voice.

"Sorry to bother you." Grant and Anna stood in the doorway, each of them carrying two glasses of champagne. "It's almost midnight. We all thought you'd like to make a toast."

Trace looked from Grant to Anna, wondered if he

and Becca looked as sloppy in love as these two newlyweds.

Yeah, I guess we do, he thought, surprised he didn't mind at all.

They joined the others and when midnight struck, there were cheers and kisses throughout the room. Holding Becca's hand, Trance stepped to the center of the room.

He lifted his glass. "To family."

"To family," they replied, then clinked glasses and drank.

He had no idea what the new year would bring, but one thing was certain, he thought as he pulled Becca close and glanced around the room.

It wouldn't be boring.

* * * * *

Silhouette®

Desire

COMING NEXT MONTH

#1699 BILLIONAIRE'S PROPOSITION—Leanne Banks
Battle for the Boardroom
He wants to control a dynasty. She just wants his baby. Who will outmaneuver whom?

#1700 ENGAGEMENT BETWEEN ENEMIES—Kathie DeNosky
The Illegitimate Heirs
Sometimes the only way to gain the power you desire is to marry your enemy.

#1701 THE MAN MEANS BUSINESS—Annette Broadrick
Business was his only agenda, until his loyal assistant decided to make marriage hers!

#1702 THE SINS OF HIS PAST—Roxanne St. Claire
Did paying for his sins mean leaving the only woman he wanted…for a second time?

#1703 HOUSE CALLS—Michelle Celmer
Doctors do not make the best patients… Here's to seeing if they make the best bedmates….

#1704 THUNDERBOLT OVER TEXAS—Barbara Dunlop
She really wants a priceless piece of jewelry, but will she actually become a cowboy's bride to get it?

SDCNM1205